The dreams changed.

There were, as before, memories from the minds of the colonists who had long lived in symbiosis with the fungus but now there were other memories—brief flashes, indistinct at first but all the time increasing in clarity and duration. There were glimpses of the faces and the bodies of women whom Grimes had known.

The women . . .

And the ships.

Lines from a long-ago read and long-ago forgotten piece of verse drifted through Grimes' mind:

The arching sky is calling
Spacemen back to their trade . . .

He was sitting in the control room of his first command, a little Serpent Class courier, a king at last even though his realm, to others, was a very insignificant one. Obedient to the touch of his fingers on the console the tiny ship lifted.

All hands! Stand by! Free Falling!
The lights below us fade . . .

And through the dream, louder and louder, surged the arythmic hammering of a spaceship's inertial drive. . . .

THE
FAR
TRAVELER

A. Bertram Chandler

DAW BOOKS, INC
DONALD A. WOLLHEIM, PUBLISHER

1301 Avenue of the Americas
New York, N.Y.   10019

Dedication

To all far travelers.

FIRST PRINTING, FEBRUARY 1979

1 2 3 4 5 6 7 8 9

Chapter 1

The *Far Traveler* came to Botany Bay, to Paddington, dropping down to the Bradman Oval—which sports arena, since the landing of the Survey Service's *Discovery*, had become a spaceport of sorts. *Discovery* was gone, to an unknown destination, taking with her the mutineers and the friends that they had made on the newly discovered Lost Colony. The destroyer *Vega*, despatched from Lindisfarne Base to apprehend the mutineers, was still in the Oval, still lying on her side, inoperative until such time as the salvage tugs should arrive to raise her to the perpendicular. *Discovery*, under the command of her rebellious first lieutenant, had toppled the other ship before making her escape.

John Grimes, lately captain of *Discovery*, was still on Botany Bay. He had no place else to go. He had resigned from the Federation's Survey Service, knowing full well that with the loss of his ship his famous luck had run out, that if ever he returned to Lindisfarne he would be brought before a court martial and, almost certainly, would be held responsible for the seizure by mutineers of a valuable piece of the Interstellar Federation's property. And, in all likelihood, he would be held to blame for the quite considerable damage to *Vega*.

In some ways, however, he was still lucky. Apart from anything else he had a job, one for which he was qualified professionally if not temperamentally even though Botany Bay, as yet, owned no spaceships under its flag. (The lost-in-space *Lode Wallaby*, bringing the original colonists, had crashed on landing and, in any case, the essentially cranky gaussjammers had been obsolete for generations.) Nonetheless Botany Bay now needed a spaceport; since the news of *Discovery*'s landing had been broadcast throughout the Galaxy an influx of visitors from outside was to be expected. A spaceport must have a Port Captain. Even if Grimes had not been on more than merely friendly terms with Mavis, Lady Mayor of Paddington and President of the Planetary Council of Mayors, he would have been the obvious choice.

Obvious—but not altogether popular. *Vega's* people were still on Botany Bay and all of them blamed Grimes for the wreck of their vessel and, come to that, Commander Delamere, the destroyer's captain, had always hated Grimes' guts. (It was mutual.) And there were the parents whose daughters had flown the coop with the *Discovery* mutineers—and quite a few husbands whose wives had done likewise. Vociferously irate, too, were the cricket enthusiasts whose series of test matches had been disrupted by the cluttering up of the Oval with spaceships.

Only the prompt intervention of the local police force had saved Grimes, on one occasion, from a severe beating up at the hands of a half dozen of Delamere's Marines. There had been no police handy when a husband whose wife had deserted with *Discovery's* bo's'n gave Grimes two black eyes. And he was becoming tired of the white-clad, picketing cricketers outside his temporary office continually chanting, "Terry bastard, go home!"

Then *The Far Traveler* came to Botany Bay.

She was not a big ship but large for what she was, a deep-space yacht. Her home port—Grimes had ascertained during the preliminary radio conversations with her master—was Port Bluewater on El Dorado. That made sense. Only the filthy rich could afford space yachts—and El Dorado was known as the Planet of the Filthy Rich. Grimes had been there once, a junior officer in the Zodiac Class cruiser *Aries*. He had been made to feel like a snotty-nosed urchin from the wrong side of the tracks. He had been told, though, that he would be welcome to return—but only after he had made his first billion credits. He did not think it at all likely that he ever would return.

The Far Traveler dropped down through the clear, early morning sky, the irregular beat of her inertial drive swelling from an irritable mutter to an almost deafening clatter as she fell. The rays of the rising sun were reflected dazzlingly from her burnished hull. There was a peculiarly yellow quality to the mirrored light.

Grimes stood on the uppermost tier of the big grandstand watching her and, between times, casting an observant eye around his temporary domain. The triangle of scarlet beacons was there, well clear of the hapless *Vega*, the painfully bright flashers in vivid contrast to the dark green grass on which they stood. At the head of each of the tall flagstaffs around the Oval floated the flag of Botany Bay—blue, with red,

6

white and blue superimposed crosses in the upper canton, a lopsided cruciform constellation of silver stars at the fly.

He was joined by the Deputy Port Captain. Skipper Wheeldon was not a spaceman—yet. He had been master of one of the big dirigibles that handled most of Botany Bay's airborne commerce. But he wanted to learn and already possessed a good grasp of spaceport procedure.

He said, "She's comin' in nicely, sir."

Grimes grunted dubiously. He made a major production of filling and lighting his pipe. He said, speaking around the stem, "If I were that captain I'd be applying more lateral thrust to compensate for windage. Can't he see that he's sagging badly to leeward? If he's not careful he'll be sitting down on top of *Vega.* . ."

He raised the wrist upon which he wore the portable transceiver to his mouth—but before he could speak it seemed almost as though the yacht master had overheard Grimes' remarks to Wheeldon. The note of the inertial drive suddenly changed, the beat becoming more rapid as the incoming ship added a lateral component to her controlled descent.

She was falling slowly now, very slowly, finally hovering a scant meter above the close-cropped grass. She dropped again, almost imperceptibly. Grimes wasn't sure that she was actually down until the inertial drive was shut off. The silence was almost immediately broken by the shouts of the picketing, bat-brandishing cricketers—kept well clear of the landing area by slouch-hatted, khaki-clad police—bawling, "Terry, go home! Spacemen, go home!"

A telescopic mast extended itself from the needle prow of the golden ship. A flag broke out from its peak—dark purple and on it, in shining gold, the CR monogram. The Galactic Credit sign—and the ensign of El Dorado.

"I suppose we'd better go down to roll out the red carpet," said Grimes.

Chapter 2

Grimes stood at the base of the slender golden tower that was *The Far Traveler*, waiting for the after airlock door to open, for the ramp to be extended. With him were Wheeldon and Jock Tanner, the Paddington chief of police who, until things became properly organized, would be in charge of such matters as Customs, Immigration and Port Health formalities. And there was Shirley Townsend, the Mayor's secretary. (Mavis herself was not present. She had said, "I just might get up at sparrowfart to see a king or a queen or a president comin' in, but I'm damned if I'll put meself out for some rich bitch. . .")

"Takin' their time," complained Tanner.

"Perhaps we should have gone round to the servants' entrance," said Grimes half seriously.

The outer door of the airlock slowly opened at last and, as it did so, the ramp extruded itself, a long metal tongue stretching out to lick the dew that still glistened on the grass. Like the shell-plating of the ship it was gold—or, thought Grimes, gold-plated. Either way it was ostentatious.

A man stood in the airlock chamber to receive them. He was tall and thin, and his gorgeous uniform, festoons of gold braid on dark purple, made him look like a refugee from a Strauss operetta. His lean face bore what seemed to be a permanently sour expression. Among the other gleaming encrustations on his sleeve Grimes could distinguish four gold bands. So this had to be the captain. . . And why should the captain be doing a job—the reception of port officials—usually entrusted to, at best, a senior officer?

The yachtmaster looked down at the boarding party. He seemed to decide that Grimes—wearing a slightly modified airship captain's uniform, light blue, with four black stripes on each shoulderboard, with a cap badge on which the silver dirigible had been turned through ninety degrees to make it look like a spaceship—was in charge. He said, "Will you

8

come aboard, please? The Baroness d'Estang will receive you in her sitting room."

Grimes led the way up the ramp. He introduced himself. "Grimes, Acting Port Captain," he said, extending his hand.

"Billinger—Master *de jure* but not *de facto*," replied the other with a wry grin.

Grimes wondered what was meant by this, but discreet inquiries could be made later. He introduced his companions. Then Captain Billinger led the party into an elevator cage. He pushed no buttons—there were no buttons to push—but merely said, "Her Excellency's suite."

The locals were obviously impressed. Grimes was not; such voice-actuated mechanisms were common enough on the worlds with which he was familiar. The ascent was smooth, the stop without even the suspicion of a jolt. They disembarked into a vestibule, on to a thick-piled purple carpet that made a rich contrast to the golden bulkheads. A door before them slid silently open. Billinger led the way through it. He bowed to the tall, slim woman reclining on a *chaise longue* and announced, "The port officials, Your Excellency."

"Thank you, Captain," she replied in a silvery voice, adding, "You may go."

Billinger bowed again, then went.

Grimes looked down at the Baroness and she up at him. She was slim yet rounded, the contours of her body revealed rather than hidden by the filmy white translucency that enrobed her. There was a hint of pink-nippled breasts, of dark pubic shadow. Her cheekbones were high, her mouth wide and firm and scarlet, her chin not overly prominent but definitely firm, her nose just short of being prominent and delicately arched. Her lustrous bronze hair was braided into a natural coronet in which flashed not-so-small diamonds. Even larger stones, in ornate gold settings, depended from the lobes of her ears.

She reminded Grimes of Goya's *Maja*—the draped version—although her legs were much longer. And the furnishings of her sitting room must be like—he thought—the appointments of the boudoir in which that long ago and far away Spanish aristocrat had posed for the artist. Certainly there was nothing in these surroundings that even remotely suggested a spaceship.

He was abruptly conscious of his off-the-peg uniform, of his far from handsome face, his prominent ears. He felt these blushing hotly, a sure sign of embarrassment.

She said sweetly, "Please sit down, Acting Port Captain. I

9

assume that the rank is both *de facto* and *de jure*. . ." She smiled fleetingly. "And you, Deputy Port Captain. And you, City Constable. And, of course, Miss Townsend. . ."

"How did you. . . ?" began Shirley. (It came out as " 'Ow did yer. . . ?") "That *de facto* and *de jure* business, I mean. . ."

"I heard, and watched, the introductions at the airlock," said the Baroness, waving a slim, long hand toward what looked like a normal although ornately gold-framed mirror.

The police officer fidgeted on the edge of a spindly-legged chair that looked as though it was about to collapse, at any moment, under his weight. He said, "If you'll excuse me, Baroness, I'll go an' see the skipper about the port formalities. . ."

"They will be handled here," said the Baroness firmly. She did not actually finish the sentence with "my man" but the unspoken words hung in the faintly scented air. She went on, "I have always considered any of my business too important to be left to underlings." She clapped her hands. A man dressed in archaic servant's livery—white, frilled shirt, scarlet, brass-buttoned waiscoat, black knee-breeches, white stockings, black, gold-buckled shoes—entered silently. A man? No. He was, Grimes realized, one of those uncannily humanoid serving robots with which he had become familiar during his visit to El Dorado, years ago. He—it?—was carrying folders of documents—clearances, crew and passenger lists, declarations, store lists and manifests. Without hesitation he handed the papers to the City Constable.

"Is he *all* gold?" asked Shirley in an awed voice. "Under his clothes and all?"

"Yes," the Baroness told her. Then, speaking generally, "Will you take refreshment? There is coffee, if you wish, or tea, or wine. I know that, by your time, it is early in the day—but I have never known Spumante Vitelli to come amiss at any hour of the clock."

"Spumante Vitelli?" asked Shirley Townsend, determinedly talkative. "Sounds like an emetic. . ."

"It's an El Doradan sparkling wine," Grimes said hastily. "From Count Vitelli's vineyards."

"You know El Dorado, Port Captain?" asked the Baroness, polite but condescending surprise in her voice.

"I was there," said Grimes. "Some years ago."

"But this is a Lost Colony. You have had no facilities for space travel since the founders made their chance landing."

"Commander Grimes is out of the Federation's Survey Service," said Jock Tanner.

"Indeed?" The fine eyebrows arched over the dark violet eyes. "Indeed? *Commander* Grimes? There was—I recall—a Lieutenant Grimes. . ."

"There was," said Grimes. "Me." Then—the memories were flooding back—"You must know the Princess Marlene von Stolzberg, Your Excellency."

The Baroness laughed. "Not intimately, Port Captain or Commander. She's too much of the hausfrau, fat and dowdy, for my taste."

"Hausfrau?" echoed Grimes bewilderedly. That was not how he recalled Marlene.

"Many women change," said the Baroness, "and not always for the better when they become mothers." She went on maliciously, "And what about the father of the child? As I recall it, there was quite a scandal. You, and dear Marlene, and that mad old Duchess, and poor Henri . . . It's a small universe, John Grimes, but I never did meet you on El Dorado and I never dreamed that I should meet you here. . ."

The robot servitor was back, bearing a golden (of course) tray on which was a golden ice bucket, in it a magnum of the Spumante, and gold-rimmed, crystal goblets. He poured, serving his mistress first. Glasses of the sparkling, pale golden wine were raised in salute, sipped from.

"Not a bad drop o' plonk," said Shirley, speaking with deliberate coarseness.

Jock Tanner, doing his best to divert attention from her, put his glass down on the richly carpeted deck, picked up a sheath of the papers. "John," he said, "You know more about these things than I do. . . This clearance from Tallifer. . . Shouldn't it have been signed by the Chief Medical Officer?"

"Not necessarily," said Grimes, putting down his own glass and getting up from his chair, walking across to the police officers. "But I think we'd better get Shirley—she's used to wading through bumf—to make sure that everything has been signed by a responsible official."

"Orl right," grumbled the girl. "Orl right." She drained her glass, belched delicately, joined Grimes and Tanner. The hapless Wheeldon, out of his social depth and floundering, was left to make polite conversation with the Baroness.

Shortly thereafter *The Far Traveler* was granted her Inward Clearance and the boarding party trooped down the golden gangway to the honest turf.

11

"You do have posh friends, John," said Shirley Townsend as soon as they were down and off the ramp.

"I didn't have any friends on El Dorado," said Grimes, not altogether truthfully and with a note of bitterness in his voice.

Chapter 3

Captain Billinger was relaxing. He still looked far from happy but his long face had lost some of the lines of strain. He had changed from his fancy dress uniform into more or less sober civilian attire—a bright orange shirt tucked into a kilt displaying an improbable looking tartan in which a poisonous green predominated, highly polished scarlet kneeboots. He was sitting with Grimes at a table in the saloon bar of the Red Kangaroo.

He gulped beer noisily. "Boy," he said, "boy, oh boy! Am I ever glad to get off that rich bitch's toy ship!"

"But you're rich yourself, surely," said Grimes. "You must be, to be an El Doradan. . ."

"Ha! Me an El Doradan! That'd be the sunny Friday! No, Captain, I'm just a poor but reasonably honest Dog Star Line second mate. *Beagle* happened to be on Electra when her ladyship was there to take delivery of her super-duper yatchet. Seems that she came there in an El Doradan ship—they do have ships, you know, and a few playboy spacemen to run 'em—and assumed that she'd be allowed to lift off in her own fully automated vessel without having a qualified human master on board. But Lloyds'—may the Odd Gods of the Galaxy rot their cotton socks!—got into the act. No duly certificated master astronaut on the Register, no insurance cover. But money talks, as always. More than a couple or three Dog Star line shares are held by her high and mightiness. So the Old Man got an urgent Carlottigram from Head Office—I'd like to know what it said!—and, immediately after receipt, yelled for me and then turned on the hard sell. Not that there was any need for it. The offer of a Master's berth at well above *our* Award rates for the rank. . . Only a yachtmaster, it's true—but master nonetheless and bloody well paid. Like a mug, I jumped at it. Little did I know. . ." He slurped down the remains of his beer and waved two fingers at the near-naked, plumply attractive blonde waitress to order refills.

"So you don't like the job, Captain," said Grimes.

13

"You can say that again, Captain. And again. Cooped up with a snooty, rich bitch in a solid gold sardine can. . . ."

"Gold-plated, surely," interjected Grimes.

"No. Gold. G-O-L-D. Gold."

"But gold's not a structural material."

"It is after those eggheads on Electra have finished mucking about with it. They rearrange the molecules. Or the atoms. Or something."

"Fantastic," commented Grimes.

"The whole bloody ship's fantastic. A miracle of automation or an automated miracle. A human captain is just a figurehead. You watched the set down yesterday?"

"Of course. I am the Port Captain, you know. There was something a bit . . . odd about it. I can guess now what it must have been. The ship was coming down by herself without a human hand on the controls—and making a slight balls of it. And then *you* took over."

Billinger glared at Grimes. "Ha! Ha bloody ha! For your information, Port Captain, *I* was bringing her down. At first. Yes, I know damn well that there was drift. But I was putting on speed. At the last possible moment I was going to make a spectacular lateral hedge-hop and sit down bang in the middle of the beacons. And then *She* had to stick her tits in. 'Take your ape's paws off the controls!' she told me. 'The computer may not be as old as you—but she knows more about ship-handling than you'll ever learn in your entire, misspent life!' "

The waitress brought two fresh pots of beer. Grimes could tell by the way that she looked at Billinger that she liked him. (She knew, of course, who he was—and would assume that he, as captain of a solid gold spaceship, would be rich.)

"Thank you, dear," said Billinger. He leered up at her and she simpered sweetly down at him. She took the bank note— the Baroness had traded a handful or so of precious stones for local currency—that he handed her, began to fumble in the sequined sporran that was, apart from high-heeled sandals, her only clothing for change.

"That will be all right," said Billinger grandly.

Throwing money around like a drunken spaceman. . . thought Grimes.

"And what are you doing tonight after you close, my dear?" went on Billinger.

"If you wait around, sir, you'll find out," she promised, her simper replaced by a definitely encouraging smile.

14

She left the table reluctantly, her firm buttocks seeming to beckon as she moved away.

"I believe I'm on to something there," murmured Billinger. "I do. I really do. And I deserve it. I've been too long confined to that space-going trinket box with bitchy Micky flaunting the body beautiful all over the whole damned ship—and making it quite plain that there was nothing doing. You can look—but you mustn't touch. That's her ladyship!"

Grimes remembered his own experiences on El Dorado. He asked, however, "What exactly is she doing out here?"

"Research. Or so she says. For her thesis for a doctorate in some damn science or other. Social Evolution In The Lost Colonies. Not that she'll find much to interest her here. Not kinky enough. Mind you, this'd be a fine world for an honest working stiff like me. . ." He stiffened abruptly. "Talk of the devil. . ."

"Of *two* devils. . ." corrected Grimes.

She swept into the crowded bar-room, the gleaming length of her darkly tanned legs displayed by a skirt that was little more than a wide belt of gold mesh, topped by a blouse of the same material that was practically all decolletage. Her dark-gleaming hair was still arranged in a jewel-studded coronet. She was escorted by no less a person than Commander Frank Delamere. Handsome Frankie was attired for the occasion in mess full dress—spotless white linen, black and gold, a minor constellation of tinkling miniatures depending from rainbow ribbons on the left breast of his superbly cut jacket. They were no more than Good Attendance medals, Grimes well knew—but they looked impressive.

The handsome couple paused briefly at the table at which Grimes and Billinger were seated.

"Ah, Mr. Grimes. . ." said Delamere nastily.

"*Captain* Grimes," corrected the owner of that name.

"A civilian, courtesy title," sneered Delamere. "A. . . Port Captain."

He made it sound at least three grades lower than Spaceman, Fourth Class. (Grimes himself, come to that, had always held Port Captains in low esteem—but that was before he became one such.)

"Perhaps we should not have come here, Francis," said the Baroness.

"Why shouldn't you?" asked Grimes. "This is Liberty Hall. You can spit on the mat and call the cat a bastard." He knew that he was being childish but was deriving a perverse pleasure from the exchange.

15

"Come, Francis," she said imperiously. "I think that I see a vacant table over there. A very good night to you, Acting Port Captain. And to . . . to you, Captain Billinger? Of course. Forgive me, but I did not recognize you in your civilian finery."

She glided away. Her rear view was no less enticing than that of the waitress had been but, nonetheless, she was the sort of woman who looked and walked like an aristocrat no matter what she was or was not wearing. Delamere, a fatuous smirk on his too regularly featured face, followed.

"A lovely dollop of trollop," muttered Grimes.

Billinger scowled. "It's all very well for you, Captain," he complained, "but *I* have to work for that bitch!"

"My nose fair bleeds for you," said Grimes unfeelingly.

So Delamere was a fast worker. And Delamere, as Grimes well knew, was the most notorious womanizer in the entire Survey Service. And he *used* women. His engagement to the very plain daughter of the Admiral Commanding Lindisfarne Base had brought him undeserved promotions. But Delamere and this El Doradan baroness? That was certainly intriguing. She was a sleek, potentially dangerous cat, not a silly kitten. Who would be using whom? Grimes, back in his quarters in the mayoral palace, lay awake in the wide bed pondering matters; in spite of the large quantities of beer he had consumed he was not sleepy. He was sorry that Mavis, the Mayor, had not come to him this night as she usually did. She was well endowed with the shrewdness essential in a successful politician and he would have liked to talk things over with her.

Delamere and the Baroness. . .

The Baroness and Delamere. . .

He wished them joy of each other.

He wished Billinger and his little blonde waitress joy of each other.

But a vague premonition kept nagging at him. Something was cooking. He wished that he knew what it was.

16

Chapter 4

Two mornings later he found out.

Billinger, his face almost as purple as the cloth of his gaudy uniform, stormed into Grimes' little office atop the grandstand just as he was settling down to his morning tea, freshly brewed by Shirley who, by now, was working for him as much as for the Mayor, and hot buttered scones liberally spread with jam.

"This is too much!" yelled *The Far Traveler's* captain.

Grimes blinked, thinking at first that the other was referring to the matutinal snack. But this was unlikely, he realized. "Calm down, calm down," he soothed. "Take a pew. Have a cuppa. And a scone. . ."

"Calm down, you say? How would *you* feel in my shoes? I was engaged as a yachtmaster, not a tugmaster. I should have been consulted. But *she,* as per bloody usual, has gone over my head!"

"What is all this about?" demanded Grimes.

"You mean that you don't know either, Captain?"

"No. Sit down, have some tea and tell me all about it. Shirley—a mug for Captain Billinger, please."

"*She,*" said Billinger after a tranquilizing sip, "is rolling in money—but that doesn't inhibit her from grabbing every chance to make more of the filthy stuff. *She* has signed a contract with your pal Delamere, engaging to raise *Vega* to lift-off position. She just happened to mention it to me, casual like."

"You're not a tugmaster," agreed Grimes, "and a space-yacht is certainly not a tug. Looks to me as though she's bitten off more than she—or *you*—can chew."

"Maybe not," said Billinger slowly, "maybe not. She's a powerful little brute—*The Far Traveler,* I mean. She's engines in her that wouldn't be out of place in a battleship. But *I* should have been consulted."

"So should I," said Grimes. "So should I. After all, this is *my* spaceport, such as it is." And then, more to himself than to the other, "But Frankie won't be too popular, signing away a large hunk of the taxpayers' money when the Survey Service's own tugs are well on the way to here."

"They're not," said Billinger. "It seems that there's been some indefinite delay. Delamere got a Carlottigram about it. Or so *she* says."

"And so Frankie keeps his jets clear," murmured Grimes in a disappointed voice. "He would."

And just how would this affect *him*? he wondered. *Vega* lying helplessly on her side was one thing, *Vega* restored to the perpendicular, to the lift-off position, would be an altogether different and definitely dangerous kettle of fish. Even should her drives, inertial and reaction, require adjustments or repairs she would be able to deploy her quite considerable weaponry—her automatic cannon, missile launchers and lasers. The city of Paddington would lay at her mercy.

And then?

An ultimatum to the Mayor?

Deliver the deserter, ex-Commander Grimes, to Federation Survey Service custody so that he may be carried to Lindisfarne Base to stand trial—or else?

Grimes shrugged away his apprehensions. Handsome Frankie wouldn't dare. Botany Bay was almost in the backyard of the Empire of Waverley and, thanks to certain of *Discovery's* technicians, now possessed its own deep-space radio equipment, the Time-Space-twisting Carlotti communications and direction-finding system. A squeal to the Emperor—who'd been getting far too uppish of late—and Imperial Navy cruisers would be piling on the lumes to this sector of space. There would be all the makings of a nasty interstellar incident with Frankie having to carry the can back. And, in any case, H.I.M.S. *Robert Bruce* was already en route to Botany Bay to show the Thistle Flag.

But what was Billinger saying?

". . . interesting problem, all the same. It wouldn't be so bad if she'd let me handle it. But not her. It'll either be that bloody computer or that popinjay of an FSS commander, or the pair of 'em working in collusion. With *her* sticking her tits into everything, as always."

"And, of course," Grimes pointed out just to cheer him up, "you, as master, will be legally responsible if anything goes wrong."

"Don't I know it! For two pins I'd resign. I'd be quite happy waiting here for another ship to come along; after all, I've a pile of credits due in back pay." He got to his feet.

"Oh, well, I suppose I'd better get back to my noble vessel to see what else has been cooked up in my absence."

"I'll come with you," said Grimes.

The pair of them stood in the Baroness' boudoir like two schoolboys summoned before a harsh headmistress. She did not ask them to sit down. And she, herself, was not reclining decoratively on her chaise longue but seated at a *secrétaire*, a gracefully designed desk—excellent reproduction or genuine antique?—with rich ormolu decoration. It must be, thought Grimes, a reproduction. His mind was a repository for scraps of useless knowledge and he remembered that the original ormolu had been brass imitating gold. Only the genuine precious metal would do for the Baroness.

She looked up from the papers before her. A pair of heavy, old-fashioned spectacles, black-framed, went oddly with her filmy gown—but somehow suited her. She said, "Captain Billinger, I believe that you, as master, are required to affix your signature to this document, this contract. I, as owner, have already signed."

Sulkily Billinger went to stand by the ornate desk, produced a stylus from the breast pocket of his uniform, bent to scribble his name.

"And Port Captain Grimes. . . I understand that I should ask your permission to engage in towage—if that is the correct word—within the spaceport limits."

"That is so, Your Excellency," said Grimes.

"I assume that the permission is granted."

Grimes was tempted to say no but decided against it. Commander Delamere represented the Survey Service and the Baroness d'Estang represented El Dorado, with its vast wealth and influence. There are times—and this was one of them—when it is futile to fart against thunder.

He said, "Yes."

"Good. No doubt you gentlemen feel that you are entitled to be apprised as to what has been arranged between Commander Delamere and myself. The commander will supply the towing wires from his stores. It will be necessary to pierce *The Far Traveler's* shell plating about the stern to secure the towing lugs. I am informed that the welding of steel onto gold is impracticable—and, of course, the modified gold that was used to build the ship on Electra is unobtainable here. Commander Delamere assures me, however, that his artificers will be able to make good the hull after the job has been completed. All dust and shavings will be carefully collected and

19

melted down to plug the holes." She turned in her chair to address Billinger. "All relevant data has been fed into the computer." She permitted herself a smile. "You will be pleased to learn, Captain, that she does not feel herself competent to undertake what is, in effect, salvage work. Her programmers back on Electra did not envisage any circumstances such as those that have arisen now." She looked positively happy. "The guarantee has not yet expired, so I shall be entitled to considerable financial redress from Electronics and Astronautics, Incorporated." She paused, looked quizzically at Grimes, the heavy spectacles making her look like a schoolmistress condescending to share a joke with one of her pupils. "Commander Delamere did suggest that he assume temporary command of my ship during the operation but I decided not to avail myself of his kind offer."

She's shrewd, thought Grimes. *She's got him weighed up.*

She turned again to Billinger. "*You* are the master, Captain. I am paying you a handsome salary. I expect you to begin earning it. And I am sure that Port Captain Grimes will be willing to oversee the entire exercise from the ground."

"I shall be pleased to, Your Excellency," said Grimes.

"Your pleasure," she told him, "is of little consequence. After all, this is your spaceport, even though it is normally used for archaic Australian religious rites. Thank you, gentlemen."

They were dismissed.

Chapter 5

"I don't like it, John," said Mavis.

The Lady Mayor of Paddington, President of the Council of Mayors of Botany Bay, was sprawled in an easy chair in Grimes' sitting room, regarding him solemnly over the rim of her beer mug. She was a big woman, although too firm-bodied to be considered obese, older than him but still sexually attractive. She was wearing a gaudy sarong that displayed her deeply tanned, sturdy legs almost to the crotch, that left bare her strong but smooth arms and shoulders. Her lustrous, almost white hair made a startling contrast to the warm bronze of her face, as did the pale gray eyes, the very serious eyes. Of late she had been too much the mother and too little the lover for Grimes' taste.

He said, "We have to get that bloody *Vega* off your cricket pitch some time."

She said, "That's as may be—but I wouldn't trust your cobber Delamere as far as I could throw him."

"No cobber of mine," Grimes assured her. "He never was and never will be." He laughed. "Anyhow, *you* could throw him quite a fair way."

She chuckled. "An' wouldn't I like to! Right into one o' those stinkin' tanks out at the sewage farm!"

Grimes said, "But he'd never dare to use his guns to threaten you, to demand that you turn me over to him. He knows damn well that if he sparked off an incident he'd be as much in the shit with the Survey Service as I am."

She did not need to be a telepath to sense his mood. She said softly, "That Service of yours has been more a mistress—and a mother—to you than I have ever been, ever could be."

"No," he said, after too long a pause. "Not so."

"Don't lie to me, John. Don't worry about hurtin' my feelings. I'm just an old bag who's been around for so long that emotionally I'm mostly scar tissue. . ." She lit one of the cigars rolled from the leaves of the mutated tobacco of

21

Botany Bay, deeply inhaled the fragrant, aphrodisiac smoke, exhaled. Grimes, whether he wanted to or not, got his share of the potent fumes. In his eyes she became more and more attractive, Junoesque. The sarong slipped to reveal her big, firm, brown-gleaming breasts with their erect, startlingly pink nipples. He got up from his own chair, took a step toward her.

But she hadn't finished talking. Raising a hand to fend him off she said, "An' it's not only the Service. It's space itself. I've been through this sorta thing before. My late husband was a seaman—an' he thought more o' the sea an' his blasted ships than he ever did o' me. An' the airship skippers are just as bad, their wives tell me. Sea, Air an' Space. . . The great mistresses with whom we mere human women can never compete. . .

"You don't haveter tell me, Johnnie boy, but you're pinin'. It's a space-goin' command you really want, not the captaincy of a cricket field that just happens to be cluttered up with spaceships. I wish I could help—but it'll be years before we have any spaceships of our own. An' I wish I could get you off Botany Bay—for your sake, not mine! I hear things an' I hear of things. That Delamere was sayin'—never mind who to—'The Survey Service has a long arm'—an' if that bastard Grimes thinks he's safe here, he's got another thing comin'. . .' "

"Delamere!" sneered Grimes.

"He's a weak man," said Mavis, "but he's vain. An' cunning as a shit-house rat. An' dangerous."

"He couldn't fight his way out of a paper bag," said Grimes.

"He has men—an' he'll soon have a ship—to do his fightin' for him," Mavis said.

"It's up to me whether he has a ship or not," said Grimes. "And now let's forget about him, shall we?"

He dropped the last of his clothing to the floor. She was ready for him, enveloped him in her ample, warm embrace. For a time—if only for a short time—he forgot space and ships and, even, that nagging premonition of disasters yet to come.

Chapter 6

Grimes stood with Wheeldon on the close-cropped grass of the Oval—the groundsmen were still carrying out their duties although no one knew when, if ever, play would be resumed—a scant five meters from the recumbent hulk of *Vega*. She was no more than a huge, useless, metal tube, pointed at one end and with vanes at the other. It did not seem possible that she would ever fly, had ever flown. Like a giant submarine, improbably beached on grassland, she looked—a submarine devoid of conning tower and control surfaces. Grimes remembered a visit he had paid to one of the ship-building yards on Atlantia where he, with other Survey Service officers, had witnessed the launching of a big, underseas oil tanker. And this operation, of which he was in charge, was a launching of sorts. . .

Forward of the crippled destroyer stood *The Far Traveler,* a fragile seeming golden tower, a gleaming spire supported by the flying buttresses that were her stern vanes. Between each of these there was a steel towing lug, the dull gray of the base metal contrasting harshly with the rich, burnished yellow of the yacht's shell plating. Grimes had inspected these fittings and, reluctantly, had admitted that Delamere's artificers had made a good job. To each of the three lugs was shackled a length of wire rope, silvery metal cordage that, in spite of its apparent flimsiness, was certified to possess a safe working load measured in thousands of tons. It, like the Baroness's yacht, was a product of Electra, yet another example of arcane metallurgical arts and sciences. It was hellishly expensive—but when it came to the supply of stores and equipment to its ships the Survey Service had occasional spasms of profligacy. That wire must have been in *Vega's* storerooms for years. Nobody had dreamed that it would ever be used.

Lugs had been welded to the destroyer's skin just abaft the circular transparencies of the control-room viewports. To each of these a length of the superwire was shackled. All three towlines were still slack, of course, and would be so until *The Far Traveler* took the strain. Grimes didn't much care for the setup. The problem would be to maintain an equal stress on all parts. He would have liked to have installed self-tensioning winches in either the yacht or the warship but, although such devices were in common use by Botany Bay's shipping, none were available capable of coping with the enormous strains that would be inevitable in an operation of this kind. As it was, he must do his damnedest to ensure that at least two of the wires were taking the weight at all times, and that there were no kinks. He could visualize all too clearly what would happen if there were—a broken end whipping through the air with all the viciousness of a striking snake, decapitating or bloodily bisecting anybody unlucky enough to be in the way. And he, Grimes, was liable to be one such. He had to direct things from a position where he could see at once if anything was going wrong. Delamere and the Baroness and all *Vega's* crew, with the exception of one engineer officer, were watching from the safety of the stands. And Mavis, with her entourage, was also getting a grandstand view. . .

He stood there, capless in the warm sunshine but wearing a headset with throat microphone. It was a good day for the job, he thought, almost windless. Nothing should go wrong. But if everything went right—there was that nagging premonition back again—then things could start going wrong. For him. *Heads you win, tails I lose. . .?* Maybe.

He said to Wheeldon, "Better get up to the stands. If one of those wires parts it won't be at all healthy around here."

"Not on your sweet Nelly," replied the Deputy Port Captain. "I'm supposed to be your apprentice. I want to see how this job is done."

"As you please," said Grimes. If Wheeldon wished to share the risk that was his privilege. He actuated his transceiver. "Port Captain to *Far Traveler*. Stand by."

"Standing by," came Billinger's voice in the headset.

"Port Captain to *Vega*. Stand by."

"Standing by," replied the engineer in the destroyer's inertial drive room.

Ships, thought Grimes, *should be fitted with inertial drive units developing sufficient lateral thrust to cope with this sort of situation. But I'll use whatever thrust Frankie's engineer can give me. . .*

"Port Captain to *Far Traveler*. Lift off!"

The yacht's inertial drive started up, cacophonous in the

24

still air. She lifted slowly. The wire cables started to come clear of the grass.

"Hold her at that, Billinger. Hold her. . . Now. . . Cant her, cant her. . . Just five degrees short of the critical angle. . ."

The Far Traveler was not only a floating tower, hanging twenty meters clear of the ground, but was becoming a leaning tower, toppling slowly and deliberately until her long axis was at an angle of forty degrees from the vertical. Billinger should have had no trouble holding her in that position. In a normal vessel anxious officers and petty officers would be sweating over their controls; in the fully-automated yacht servo-mechanisms would be doing all the work.

"Port Captain to *Vega*. . . Maximum lateral thrust, directed *down*!"

The destroyer came to life, snarling, protesting. The combined racket from the two ships was deafening.

"Lift her, Billinger. Lift her! Maintain your angle. . ."

The Far Traveler lifted. The cables—two of them—tautened. They . . . *thrummed*, an ominous note audible even above the hammering of the inertial drive units. But the sharp stem of *Vega* was coming clear of the grass, a patch of dead, crushed, dirty yellow showing in sharp contrast to the living green.

"Thirty-five degrees, Billinger. . ."

The change in the yacht's attitude was almost imperceptible but the threatening song of the bar-taut wires was louder.

"Increase your thrust if you can, *Vega*!"

"I'll bugger my innie if I do. . ."

"It's not *my* innie," growled Grimes. *"Increase your thrust!"*

More dead yellow was showing under the warship.

"Billinger—thirty degrees. . . Twenty-five. . . And roll her. . . Roll her to port. . . Just a touch. . . Hold it!"

For a moment it seemed that all the weight would be on one cable only but now two had the strain once more.

"Billinger! Twenty degrees. . ."

Vega was lifting nicely, coming up from the long depression that she had made with her inert tonnage. Grimes noticed worm-like things squirming among the dead grass stems—but this was no time for the study of natural history. He was trying to estimate the angle made by the destroyer's long axis with the ground. Soon he would be able to tell the engineer to apply a component of fore-and-aft thrust. . .

"Billinger, ten degrees. . ."

25

Then it happened. One of the taut wires snapped, about halfway along its length. The broken ends whipped viciously—the upper one harmlessly but the lower one slashing down to the grass close to where Grimes was standing. It missed him. He hardly noticed it.

"Billinger, roll to starboard! Roll!" He had to get the weight back on to two wires instead of only one. "Hold her! And lift! Lift!"

Would the cables hold?

"*Vega*! Fore and aft thrust! Now!"

The destroyer, her sharp bows pointing upward and rising all the time, surged ahead. Two of her stern vanes gouged long, ugly furrows in the grass. There should have been a spaceman officer in her control room to take charge of her during these final stages of the operation—but Delamere, when Grimes had raised this point, had insisted that it would not be necessary. (The obvious man for the job, of course, would have been *Vega's* captain—and Frankie, as Grimes well knew, was always inclined to regard the safety of his own skin as of paramount importance.)

Vega lifted, lifted, coming closer and closer to the vertical. Two of her vanes were in contact with the ground, the third was almost so. Grimes looked up to the taut cables. He could see bright strands of broken wire protruding from one of them. It would be a matter of seconds only before it parted, as had the first one. Obviously those safe working load certificates had been dangerously misleading. . .

"*Vega*! Full lateral thrust! Now!"

"The innie's flat out!"

Damn all engineers! thought Grimes. At crucial moments their precious machinery was always of greater importance to them than the ship.

"Double maximum thrust—or you've had it!"

The officer must have realized at last that this was an emergency. The destroyer's inertial drive not only hammered but . . . *howled*. The ship shuddered and teetered and then, suddenly, lifted her forward end, so rapidly that for an instant the cables hung slack. But Billinger quickly took the weight again and gave one last, mighty jerk. The stranded cable parted but the remaining towline held. The broken end slashed down to the grass on the other side of the destroyer from Grimes.

Vega came to the perpendicular and stood there, rocking slightly on her vanes.

"Billinger—'vast towing! *Vega*—cut inertial drive!"

26

"It's cut itself. . ." said *Vega's* engineer smugly.

And then, only then, was Grimes able to look down to see what the end of the first snapped cable had done. He stared, and swallowed, and vomited. He stood there, retching uncontrollably, befouling his clothing. But it didn't much matter. His footwear and lower legs were already spattered with blood and tatters of human flesh. The flying wire had cut the unfortunate Wheeldon—not very neatly—in two.

So Captain Billinger gingerly brought *The Far Traveler* to a landing, careful not to get the yacht's stern foul of the remaining tow wire. So Commander Delamere, at the head of his crew, his spacemen and Marines, marched down from the grandstand and across the field to resume possession of his ship. So an ambulance drove up to collect what was left of the Deputy Port Captain while Grimes stood there, staring down at the bloodied grass, retching miserably.

To him came Mavis, and Shirley and, surprisingly, the Baroness.

Mavis whispered, "It could have happened to you. . ."

Grimes said, "It should have happened to me. I was in charge. I should have checked those wires for deterioration."

The Baroness said, "I shall arrange for more than merely adequate compensation to be paid to Captain Wheeldon's relatives."

"Money!" flared Mavis. "It's all that you and your kind ever think of! If you hadn't grabbed the chance of makin' a few dollars on the side by usin' your precious yacht as a tugboat this would never've happened!"

The Baroness said, "I am sorry. Believe me, I'm sorry. . ."

"Look!" cried Shirley, pointing upward.

They looked. Ports had opened along *Vega's* sleek sides, in the plating over turrets and sponsons. The snouts of weapons, cannon and laser projectors, protruded, hunting, like the questing antennae of some giant insect.

"Here it comes," said Mavis glumly. "The ulti-bloody-matum. Give us Grimes—or else. . ." She stiffened. "But I'm not giving any cobber o' mine to those Terry bastards!"

Yet there was no ultimatum, no vastly amplified voice roaring over the sports arena. The guns ceased their restless motion but were not withdrawn, however.

"Just Frankie making sure that everything's in working order," said Grimes at last.

"Leave him to play with his toys," said Mavis. "Come on home an' get cleaned up." She turned to the El Doradan woman. "You comin' with us, Baroness?" The tone of her voice made it obvious that she did not expect the invitation to be accepted.

"No, thank you, Your Ladyship. I must go aboard my yacht to see what must be done to make her spaceworthy again."

"C'm'on," said Mavis to Grimes and Shirley.

They walked slowly toward the main gates. All at once they were surrounded by a mob of men clad in white flannel with absurd little caps on their heads, with gaudily colored belts supporting their trousers, brandishing cricket bats.

"Terry bastard go home!" they chanted. "Terry bastard go home!"

I've got no home to go to, thought Grimes glumly.

"Bury the bastard in the holes he dug in our cricket pitch!" yelled somebody.

"Burying's too good!" yelled somebody else. "Cut 'im in two, same as he did Skipper Wheeldon!"

"It was an accident!" shouted Mavis. "Now, away with yer! Let us through!"

"I'm chocker takin' orders from you, you fat cow!" growled a man who seemed to be the ringleader, a hairy, uncouth brute against whom Grimes, in any circumstances at all, would have taken an instant dislike. "An' as it's too long ter wait for the next election. . ."

He raised his bat.

From *Vega* came a heavy rattle of automatic fire and the sky between the ship and the mob was suddenly brightly alive with tracer. Had the aim not been deliberately high there would have been sudden and violent death on the ground. Again the guns fired, and again—then Grimes and the two women found themselves standing safe and no longer molested while the cricketers bolted for cover. Three bats and a half dozen or so caps littered the trampled grass.

"An' *now* what?" asked Mavis in a shaken voice.

"Just Frankie, as a good little Survey Service commander, rallying to the support of the civil authority," said Grimes at last. Then—"But where the hell were *your* police?"

"That big, bearded bastard," muttered Mavis, "just happens to be a senior sergeant. . ."

Then Tanner, with a squad of uniformed men, arrived belatedly to escort the mayoral party to the palace. The City Constable was neither as concerned nor as apologetic as he should have been.

Chapter 7

The next day was a heavy one for Grimes.

There were, as yet, no Lloyd's Surveyors on Botany Bay; nonetheless *The Far Traveler* was required to have a fresh Certificate of Spaceworthiness issued to her before she could lift from the surface of the planet. Of course, the Baroness could depart without such documentation if she so wished— but without it her ship would not be covered by the underwriters. And she was, for all her title and air of elegant decadence, a shrewd businesswoman.

She called Grimes to her presence. The robot butler ushered him into the lady's boudoir where she, flimsily clad as usual, was seated at her beautiful, fragile-seeming, pseudo-antique desk. She was wearing the heavy-rimmed spectacles again, was studying a thick, important-looking book.

"Ah, good morning, Acting Port Captain. . . Now, this matter of insurance. . . As you already know, Commander Delamere's artificers were obliged to pierce my hull to fit the towing lugs. Today they are making the damage good as required by the contract. After these repairs have been completed a survey must be carried out."

"By whom, Your Excellency?" asked Grimes.

"By you, of course, Port Captain. You will receive the usual fee."

"But I'm not a surveyor. . ."

"You are the Port Captain." A slim index finger tipped with a long, gold-enamelled nail stabbed down at the open pages. "Listen. *On planets where Lloyd's maintain neither offices, agents nor surveyors Lloyd's Certificates may be endorsed or issued by such planetary officials as are deemed competent by the Corporation to carry out such functions. Port Captains, Port Engineers, etc., etc. . . . . Commanding officers of vessels or bases of the Interstellar Federation's Survey Service. . ."* She smiled briefly. "I have no intention of paying a surveyor's fee to your friend Commander Delamere. In any case, as his people are making the repairs he is ruled

29

out." She read more. *"Commanding officers of vessels or bases of the Imperial Navy of Waverley.* No, I'm not going to wait around until that Waverley cruiser—*Robert Bruce,* isn't it?—condescends to drop in. So. . ."

"So I'm it," said Grimes.

"Elegantly expressed, Acting Port Captain. But I suggest that you accept guidance from the computer. After all, she is the ship's brain. She *is* the ship—just as your intelligence is *you*—and is fully capable of self diagnosis."

"Mphm," grunted Grimes. He wanted to pull his vile pipe out of his pocket, to fill it and light it, but knew that to ask permission so to do would bring a rebuff. He said, "So you need a Lloyd's Surveyor as much—or as little—as you need a captain."

She said, "I need neither—but Lloyd's of London insist that I must have both. And now may I suggest that you get on with your surveying?"

Bitch, thought Grimes. *Rich bitch. Rich, spoiled bitch.* He said, "Very well, Your Excellency," bowed stiffly and left her presence.

The humanoid robot in butler's livery led him to the elevator. The upward ride was such a short one that it would have been far less trouble to have used the spiral staircase that ornately entwined the axial shaft. Billinger was waiting in his own quarters for Grimes.

The yachtmaster was not uncomfortably housed; masters of Alpha Class liners or captains of Zodiac Class cruisers would not have complained about such accommodation. The keynote was one of masculine luxury—deep armchairs upholstered in genuine black leather, a low, glass-topped coffee table standing on sturdy, ebony legs, bookshelves all along one bulkhead, well stocked with volumes in gilt and maroon leather bindings, a gold and ebony liquor cabinet, a huge playmaster encased in gold-trimmed paneling of the same expensive timber. Holograms glowed on the other bulkheads—bright windows looking out on seascapes and mountainscapes and, inevitably, an Arcadian beach scene with the inevitable sun-bronzed, sun-bleached blonde in the foreground."

"She does you well, Captain," commented Grimes.

"Careful, Captain," said Billinger. "Big Sister is watching. And listening." He gestured toward the playmaster, the screen of which seemed to be dead. "Coffee?"

"Please."

Almost immediately a girl, a stewardess, came in, carrying a tray. It was a golden tray, of course, with golden coffee pot, cream jug and sugar bowl, gold-chased china. And the girl was also golden, wearing a short-skirted black uniform over a perfectly proportioned body that gleamed metallically.

She set the tray on the table, lifted the pot and poured. "Sugar, sir?" she asked. "Cream?"

The mechanical quality of her golden voice was barely discernible.

"Quite a work of art," remarked Grimes when she was gone.

"I'd sooner have something less good-looking in soft plastic," said Billinger coarsely. "But I've been making up for lost time on this world! Too bloody right—as the natives say—I have!"

"Big Sister. . ." murmured Grimes, looking meaningfully toward the playmaster.

"So what?" demanded Billinger belligerently. "I'm human, not a mess of printed circuits and fluctuating fields. It took humans to handle the raising of *Vega*, not the bastard off-spring of an electronic calculator and a library bank!"

"The *first* time, Captain Billinger," said a cold, mechanical yet somehow feminine voice from the playmaster. "But should a set of similar circumstances arise in the future I shall be quite capable of handling operations myself."

"Big Sister?" asked Grimes.

"In person," growled Billinger. "Singing and dancing."

"For your information, gentlemen," went on the voice, "the artificers from the destroyer have now commenced work on my stern. I would have preferred to carry out the work with my own GP robots but Her Excellency maintained that Commander Delamere must adhere to the terms of the contract. Be assured, however, that I am keeping the workmen under close observation and shall not tolerate any shoddy workmanship."

"Even so," said Grimes, "we had better go down and see what's happening."

"That will not be necessary, Acting Port Captain. I shall not lift from this planet until I am completely satisfied as to my spaceworthiness."

"*I* shall be signing the certificate, not you," said Grimes harshly.

He drained his cup—he would have liked more of that excellent coffee but this uppity robot was spoiling his enjoyment of it—put it back on the table with a decisive clatter, got to his feet.

"Coming, Billinger?" he asked.

"Yes," said he yachtmaster.

The two men made their way to the axial shaft, to the waiting elevator, and made a swift descent to the after airlock.

Vega's technicians were working under one of the destroyer's engineer lieutenants. This officer turned his head as Grimes and Billinger came down the ramp, straightened up reluctantly and accorded them a surly salute. He knew Grimes, of course, and like all of *Vega's* personnel blamed him for what had happened to that ship. He did not know Billinger, nor did he much want to.

Grimes watched the artificers at work. Scaffolding had been erected under *The Far Traveler's* stern, a light but strong framework of aluminum rods and plates. Power cables snaked over the trampled grass from the destroyer to the equipment in use. That seemed odd. Surely it would have been less trouble to use the output from the yacht's generators for the drilling, cutting and welding. He said as much to Billinger.

The engineer overheard. He said bitterly, "*She* wouldn't allow it. . ."

"The Baroness?" asked Grimes.

"No. Not her. It's not her voice that's doing all the yapping. Some other . . . lady. He raised his own voice an octave in not very convincing mimicry. " 'Why should *I* supply the power to repair the damage that *you* have done to me? Why should I wear out *my* generators?' " He paused. "And that's not the worst of it. She hasn't actually showed herself but she must have spy eyes planted, and concealed speakers. Nag, nag, nag. . ."

The voice came from nowhere, everywhere. Grimes had heard it before, in Billinger's cabin. "Careful, you men. Careful. I'm not some dirty great battleship that you're patching up. I take pride in *my* appearance, even if you take none in yours. I shall expect that scratch filled and then buffed to a mirror finish."

"Who the hell *is* she?" demanded the lieutenant.

"Big Sister," Billinger told him, his voice smug and almost happy.

"Big Sister? She sounds more like some wives I've heard."

"Not mine," said Billinger. "Not mine. Not that I've ever had one—but when I do she'll not be like that."

"They never are," said the other philosophically, "until after you've married them."

"Captain Billinger, may I suggest that you abandon this futile discussion and take some interest in the repairs? And Mr. Verity, please supervize the activities of those ham-handed apes of yours. I distinctly said that each plug must be machined to a tolerance of one micromillimeter or less. I will *not* accept ugly cracks filled in with clumsy welding."

"It's all very well," expostulated the engineer, "but *we* don't carry a stock of that fancy gold your ship is built from. We *could* use ordinary gold—but you've already said that that won't do."

"And what happened to the metal that your men drilled out?"

"There were . . . losses. There are always losses."

And how many of Vega's mechanics, wondered Grimes, *will be giving pretty little trinkets to their popsies back on Lindisfarne?*

"Very well," said the voice of the computer-pilot. "I shall supply you with gold. Please wait at the foot of the ramp."

The men waited. A female figure appeared in the after airlock and then walked gracefully down the gangway. It was Billinger's robot stewardess. The spacemen whistled wolfishly until, suddenly, they realized that she was not human. One of them muttered, "Be a bleeding shame to melt *her* down. . ."

She was carrying a golden tray and on it a teapot of the same metal, a milk jug and a sugar bowl. Wordlessly she handed these to one of the artificers.

"*My* tea service!" exclaimed Billinger.

"Nothing aboard me is yours, Captain," Big Sister told him. "As long as you are employed you are allowed the use of certain equipment."

"What *is* all this?" asked the engineer.

"Just do as *she* says," muttered Billinger. "Melt down my teapot and make it snappy. Otherwise she'll be having the buttons and braid off my uniform. . ."

Grimes wandered away. The atmosphere around the stern of the yacht was becoming heavily charged with acrimony and he was, essentially, a peace-loving man. He was careful not to walk too close to the towering *Vega.* He had no reason to like that ship and, most certainly, her captain did not like him. He sensed that he was being watched. He looked up but could see nothing but the reflection of the morning sun from the control room viewports—yet he could imagine Delamere there, observing his every move through high-powered binoculars.

"Port Captain! Hey! Port Captain!"

33

Grimes sighed. There was a small crowd of pestilential cricketers under the destroyer's quarter. What were the police doing? They were supposed to be keeping the field clear of demonstrators. But these men, he saw with some relief, were carrying neither flags nor placards although they were attired in the white uniform of their sport. He walked slowly to where they were standing.

"Wotcher doin' about this, Port Captain?" asked their leader. It was the man whom Mavis had identified as a police sergeant.

This was the too deep furrows that had been gouged in the turf by the stern vanes of the destroyer during the lifting operation.

Grimes looked at the ugly wounds in the skin of the planet. They were minor ravines rather than mere trenches. The sportsmen looked at him.

He said, "These will have to be filled. . ."

"Who by, Port Captain, who by? Tell us that."

"The groundsmen, I suppose. . ."

"Not bloody likely. You Terries did it. You can bloody well undo it. An' the sooner the bloody better."

"The sooner they're off our world the better," growled one of the other men.

"Mphm," grunted Grimes. He, too, was beginning to think that the sooner he was off this world the better. He was the outsider who, by his coming, had jolted Botany Bay out of its comfortable rut. He had friends, good friends, the Lady Mayor and those in her immediate entourage—and that was resented by many. This same resentment might easily cost Mavis the next election.

"Wotcher doin' about it?" demanded again the bearded policeman.

"I'll see Commander Delamere," promised Grimes, "and ask him to put his crew to work filling these . . . holes."

"*Ask* him, Port Captain? You'll bloody tell him."

"All right," said Grimes. "I'll tell him."

He walked away from the glowering men. He paused briefly at the foot of *Vega's* ramp, looked up at the smartly uniformed Marine on gangway duty in the airlock. The man looked down at him. His expression was hostile. *I'd better not go aboard*, thought Grimes. *I'll call* Vega *from my office.* He carried on to the grandstand, made his way up the steps to the shed that was grandiosely labelled SPACEPORT ADMINISTRATION.

He accepted the cup of tea that Shirley poured for him,

went to the telephone and punched the number that had been alloted to *Vega*. The screen lit up and the face of a bored looking junior officer appeared. "FSS *Vega*."

"Port Captain here. Could I speak to Commander Delamere?"

"I'll put you through to the control room, sir."

The screen flickered, went blank, lit up again. Delamere's face looked out from it. "Yes, Grimes? What do you want? Make it snappy; I'm busy."

"The local cricket club is concerned about the damage to their field."

"And what am *I* supposed to do about it?"

"Send some men down with shovels to fill the gashes your stern vanes cut in the turf."

"My men are spacemen, not gardeners."

"Even so, the damage has to be made good, Delamere."

"Not by me it won't be, Grimes. You're supposed to be the Port Captain and this bloody Oval is supposed to be the spaceport. Its maintenance is *your* concern."

"The maintenance of friendly relations with the natives of any world is the concern of any Survey Service commanding officer. Sending your crew to fill in the holes comes under that heading."

"*You* did that damage, Grimes, by your mishandling of the raising operation. If it's beneath your dignity to take a shovel in your own hands I suggest that you ask your new girlfriend for the loan of a few of her GP robots."

"*My* new girlfriend? I thought. . ."

Delamere scowled. "Then think again! You're welcome to the bitch, Grimes!"

The screen went blank.

Grimes couldn't help laughing. So here at last was a woman impervious to Handsome Frankie's charms. And Delamere, being Delamere, would automatically blame Grimes for his lack of success. Meanwhile—just what was the legal situation regarding the damage to the turf?

Grimes stopped laughing. It looked very much as though he would be left holding the baby.

Chapter 8

So the day went, a long succession of annoyances and frustrations. He succeeded in obtaining another audience with the Baroness—his new girlfriend, indeed!—and requested her assistance to fill the trenches. She refused. "My dear Port Captain, my robots are programmed to be personal servants and, to a limited degree, spacemen, not common laborers. Would you use your toothbrush to scrub a deck?"

If it were the only tool available, thought Grimes, he might have to do just that.

He returned to his office, called Mavis. She was short with him. She said, "I know I'm the Mayor, John, but the damage to the cricket pitch is your responsibility. You'll just have to do the best you can."

Finally he went back to *The Far Traveler*. The repair work had been completed but he thought that he had better go through the motions of being a Lloyd's Surveyor, even though it was almost impossible to detect where the golden hull had been patched, even though Big Sister had expressed her grudging satisfaction. He told the engineer lieutenant not to dismantle the staging until he had made his inspection. He tapped all around the repairs with a borrowed hammer, not at all sure what he was looking or listening for. He told the engineer to send to the destroyer for a can of vactest and then to have the black, viscous paste smeared all over the skin where the plugs had been inserted. Big Sister complained (she would) that this was not necessary, adding that she was quite happy with the making good of the damage and that she objected to having this filthy muck spread over her shell plating. Grimes told her that *he* would be signing the certificate of spaceworthiness and that he would not do so until *he* was happy.

Sulkily Big Sister pressurized the after compartment. Not the smallest air bubble marred the gleaming surface of the vactest. The artificers cleaned the gummy mess off the golden skin, began to take down the scaffolding. Grimes went aboard the ship to endorse the Lloyd's Certificate of Spaceworthiness. The Baroness was almost affable, inviting him to have a drink. Billinger was conspicuous by his absence.

The aristocrat said, looking at him over the rim of her goblet of Spumante, "This is a boring world, Captain Grimes. I know that Captain Billinger has not found it so, but there is nothing for me here."

Grimes could not resist the temptation. "Not even Commander Delamere?" he asked.

Surprisingly she took no offense. She even laughed. "Commander Delamere may think that he is the gods' own gift to womankind but I do not share that opinion. But you, Captain. . . You, with your background. . . Don't you find Botany Bay just a little boring?"

"No," said Grimes loyally. (The Baroness must surely know about Mavis and himself.) "No. . ." he repeated, after a pause. (And whom was he trying to convince?)

"Thank you, Port Captain," said the Baroness. It was clearly a dismissal.

"Thank you, Your Excellency," said Grimes.

He was escorted from the boudoir by the robot butler, taken down to the after airlock. It was already dusk, he noted. The sun was down and the sky was overcast but the breeze, what little there was of it, was pleasantly warm. He debated with himself whether or not to go up to his office to call a cab, then decided against it. It was a pleasant walk from the Oval to the Mayor's Palace, most of it through the winding streets of Paddington City. These, especially by night, held a special glamour, a gaslit magic that was an evocation of that other Paddington, the deliberately archaic enclave in the heart of bustling, towering Sydney on distant Earth.

Somehow Grimes wanted to see it all once more, to savor it. Perhaps it was a premonition. There was a conviction that sooner or later, sooner rather than later, he would be moving on.

He walked across the short grass to the main gates of the Oval. He turned to look at the two ships, both of them now floodlit—the menacing metal tower that was the destroyer, a missle of dull steel aimed at the sky, the much smaller golden spire, slender, graceful, that was the yacht. They would be gone soon, both of them—Delamere's engineers must, by now, have *Vega's* main and auxiliary machinery back in full working order and the Baroness had intimated that she had found little to interest her on Botany Bay.

They would be gone soon—and Grimes found himself wishing that he were going with them. But that was out of the question. Aboard *Vega* he would be hauled back to Lindisfarne Base to face a court martial—and he could not visualize himself aboard *The Far Traveler* with her rich bitch owner and that obnoxious electronic intelligence which Billinger had so aptly named Big Sister.

He resumed his walk, pausing once to stare up at a big dirigible that sailed overhead on its stately way to the airport, its red and green navigation lights and its rows of illuminated cabin ports bright against the darkness.

He strolled along Jersey Road, admiring the terrace houses with their beautiful cast aluminium lacework ornamenting pillars and balconies, the verdant explosions of native shrubs, darkly gleaming behind intricate white metal railings, in the front gardens. He ignored the ground car—even though this was the only traffic he had seen since leaving the spaceport—that came slowly up from behind him, its headlights throwing his long shadow before him on to the stoneflagged footpath.

He heard a voice say, "There's the bastard! Get him!"

He experienced excruciating but mercifully brief pain as the paralyzing beam of a stungun hit him and was unconscious before he had finished falling to the ground.

Chapter 9

He opened his eyes slowly, shut them again hastily. He was lying on his back, he realized, on some hard surface, staring directly into a bright, harsh light.

He heard a vaguely familiar voice say, "He's coming round now, sir."

He heard a too familiar voice reply, "Just as well, Doctor. They'll want him alive back at Base so they can crucify him."

Delamere, and his ship's surgeon. . .

He moved his head so that he would not be looking directly at the light, opened his eyes again. Delamere's classically handsome face swam into view. The man was gloating.

"Welcome aboard, Grimes," he said. "But this is not—for *you*—Liberty Hall. There's no man to spit on and if you call my ship's cat a bastard I'll have you on bread and water for the entire passage."

Grimes eased himself to a sitting posture, looked around. He was in a small compartment which, obviously, was not the ship's brig as it was utterly devoid of furniture. A storeroom? What did it matter? Delamere and the doctor stood there looking down at him. Flanking them were two Marines, their sidearms drawn and ready.

He demanded, "What the hell do you think you're playing at? Kidnapping is a crime on any planet, and I'll see that you pay the penalty!"

"Kidnapping, Grimes? You're still a Terran citizen and this ship is Terran territory. Furthermore, your . . . arrest was carried out with the assistance of certain local police officers." He smirked. "Mind you, I don't think that Her Ladyship the Mayor would approve—but she'll be told that you were last seen going down to the beach for a refreshing swim after a hard, hot day at the spaceport." He laughed. "You might kid yourself that you're a little friend to all the universe—but there's plenty of people who hate your guts."

"And you're one of them," said Grimes resignedly.

"However did you guess?" asked Delamere sardonically.

39

"I must be psychic," Grimes said.

"Save your cheap humor for the court martial, Grimes."

"If there is one, Delamere. *If* you get me back to Lindisfarne. The Mayor will know that I'm missing. She knows the sort of bastard that you are. She'll have this ship searched. . ."

Delamere laughed. "Her policemen have already boarded, looking for you. They weren't very interested but we showed them all through the accommodation, including the cells. Oh, and they did see a couple or three storerooms—but not this one. Even if they had gone as far as the outer door the radiation warning sign would have scared them off."

"Is this place hot?" asked Grimes, suddenly apprehensive.

"You'll find out soon enough," said Delamere, "when your hair starts falling out."

But Handsome Frankie, thought Grimes with relief, would never risk his own precious skin and gonads in a radioactive environment, however briefly.

Delamere looked at his watch. "I shall be lifting off in half an hour. It's a pity that I've not been able to obtain clearance from the Acting Port Captain, but in the circumstances. . ."

Grimes said nothing. There was nothing that he could say. He would never plead, not even if there was the remotest chance that Delamere would listen to him. He would save his breath for the court martial. He would need it then.

But was that muffled noise coming from the alleyway outside the storeroom? Shouting, a hoarse scream, the sound of heavy blows. . . Could it be. . . ? Could it be the police attempting a rescue after all? Or—and that would be a beautiful irony—another mutiny, this one aboard *Vega*?

He remarked sweetly, "Sounds as though you're having trouble, Frankie."

Delamere snapped to his Marines, "You, Petty and Slim! Go out and tell those men to pipe down. Place them under arrest."

"But the prisoner, sir," objected one of them.

Grimes watched indecision battling with half decisions on Delamere's face. Handsome Frankie had no desire to walk out into the middle of a free fight but he had to find out what was happening. On the other hand, he had no desire to be left alone with Grimes, even though his old enemy was unarmed and not yet recovered from the stungun blast.

There was a brief rattle of small arms fire, another hoarse scream. The Marines hastily checked their pistols—stunguns, as it happened—but seemed in no greater hurry to go out than their captain.

And then the door bulged inward—bulged until the plating around it ruptured, until a vertical, jagged-edged split appeared. Two slim, golden hands inserted themselves into the opening, took a grip and then pulled apart from each other. The tortured metal screamed, so loudly as almost to drown the crackling discharge from the Marines' stunguns.

A woman stepped through the ragged gap, a gleaming, golden woman clad in skimpy ship's stewardess's uniform. She stretched out a long, shapely arm, took the weapon from the unresisting hand of one of the Marines, squeezed. A lump of twisted, useless metal dropped with a clatter to the deck, emitted a final coruscation of sparks and an acridity of blue fumes. The other Marine went on firing at her, then threw the useless stungun into her face. She brushed it aside before it reached its target as though she were swatting a fly.

Another woman followed her, this one dressed as a lady's maid—black-stockinged, short-skirted, with white, frilly apron and white, frilly cap. She could have been a twin to the first one. She probably was. They both came from the same robot factory on Electra.

Delamere was remarkably quick on the uptake. "Piracy!" he yelled. "Action stations! Repel boarders!"

"You've two of them right here," said the supine Grimes happily. "Why don't you start repelling them?"

The stewardess spoke—but her voice was the cold voice of Big Sister. She said, "Commander Delamere, you have illegally brought Port Captain Grimes aboard your vessel and are illegally detaining him. I demand that he be released at once."

"And I demand that you get off my ship!" blustered Delamere. He was frightened and making a loud noise to hide the fact.

The stewardess brushed Delamere aside, with such force that he fetched up against the bulkhead with a bone-shaking thud. She reached down, gripped Grimes' shoulder and jerked him to his feet. He did not think that his collarbone was broken but couldn't be sure.

"Come," she said. "Or shall I carry you?"

"I'll walk," said Grimes hastily.

"Grimes!" shouted Delamere. "You're making things worse for yourself! Aiding and abetting pirates!" Then, to the Marines, "Grab him!"

They tried to obey the order but without enthusiasm. The

41

lady's maid just pushed them, one hand to each of them, and they fell to the deck.

"Doctor!" ordered Delamere. "Stop them!"

"I'm a non-combatant, Captain," said the medical officer.

There were more of the robots in the alleyway, a half dozen of them, male but sexless, naked, brightly golden. They formed up around Grimes and his two rescuers, marched toward the axial shaft. The deck trembled under the rhythmic impact of their heavy metal feet. And there were injured men in the alleyway, some unconscious, some groaning and stirring feebly. There was blood underfoot and spattered on the bulkheads. There were broken weapons that the automata kicked contemptuously aside.

Somebody was firing from a safe distance—not a laser weapon but a large caliber projectile pistol. (Whoever it was had more sense than to burn holes through his own ship from the inside—or, perhaps, had just grabbed the first firearm available.) Bullets ricocheted from bulkheads and deckhead, whistled through the air. There was the *spang!* of impact—metal on metal—as one hit the stewardess on the nape of her neck. She neither staggered nor faltered and there was not so much as a dent to mark the place.

They pressed on, with Grimes' feet hardly touching the deck as he was supported by the two robot women. There was an officer ahead of them, guarding the access to the spiral staircase that would take them down to the after airlock. Holding a heavy pistol in both hands he pumped shot after shot at the raiders and then, suddenly realizing the futility of it, turned and ran.

Down the stairway the raiding party clattered. The inner door of the airlock was closed. The two leading robots just leaned on it and it burst open. The outer door, too, was sealed and required the combined strength and weight of three of the mechanical men to force it. The ramp had been retracted and it was all of ten meters from the airlock to the ground. Two by two the robots jumped, sinking calf-deep into the turf as they landed.

"Jump!" ordered the stewardess who, with the lady's maid, had remained with Grimes.

He hesitated. It was a long way down and he could break an ankle, or worse.

"Jump!" she repeated.

Still he hesitated.

He cried out in protest as she picked him up, cradling him briefly in her incredibly strong arms, then tossed him gently

42

outboard. He fell helplessly and then six pairs of hands caught him, cushioned the impact, lowered him to the ground. He saw the two female robots jump, their short skirts flaring upward to waist height. They were wearing no underclothing. He remembered, with wry humor, Billinger's expressed preference for something in soft plastic rather than hard metal. . .

They marched across the field to *The Far Traveler*. Somebody in *Vega's* control room—Delamere?—had gotten his paws on to the firing console of the destroyer's main armament. Somebody, heedless of the consequences, was running amuk with a laser cannon—somebody, fortunately, who would find it hard to hit the side of a barn even if he were inside the building.

Well to the right a circle of damp grass exploded into steam and incandescence—and then the beam slashed down ahead of them. Perhaps it was not poor shooting but a warning shot across the bows. The lady's maid reached into a pocket of her apron, pulled out a small cylinder, held it well above her head. It hissed loudly, emitting a cloud of dense white smoke. The vapor glowed as the laser beam impinged upon it and under the vaporous umbrella the air was suddenly unbearably—but not lethally—hot. And then the induced flourescence blinked off. They were too close to the yacht and even Delamere—especially Delamere!—would realize the far-reaching consequences of a vessel owned by a citizen of El Dorado were fired upon by an Interstellar Federation's warship.

They tramped up the golden ramp, into the after airlock. Supported by the two female robots, Grimes was taken to the Baroness's boudoir. She was waiting for him there. So were Mavis, Shirley, Jock Tanner and Captain Billinger.

The yachtmaster was not in uniform.

Chapter 10

"You have to leave us, John," said Mavis regretfully. (But not regretfully enough, thought Grimes.)

"But," he objected over the cold drink that had been thrust into his hand by the Mayor.

"I can no longer guarantee your safety," she said.

"Neither can I," said Tanner. He grinned rather unpleasantly. "And Mavis, here, has to start thinkin' about the next elections."

"Your Excellency," said the robot butler, entering the room, "there is a Commander Delamere with twelve armed Marines at the after airlock. I refused them admission, of course."

"Of course," agreed his mistress. "And if he refuses to leave see to it that the general purpose robots escort him back to his ship."

"Very good, Your Excellency." (The reply came not from the butler but from the ornately gold-framed mirror. All the robots, Grimes realized, were no more than extensions of Big Sister.)

The Baroness looked at Grimes. She said, "You are fortunate. Big Sister saw you being taken aboard *Vega*. And when Her Ladyship appealed to me for aid I decided to give it. After all, we on El Dorado—or some of us—are indebted to you."

"Your Excellency. . ." It was the robot butler back. "Commander Delamere claims that our GP robots did considerable damage to his vessel and also injured several officers and ratings."

"The GP robots. . ." murmured Grimes. "And that pair of brass Amazons."

"*Golden* Amazons," the Baroness corrected him coldly. Then, to the servitor, "Tell Commander Delamere that he may sue if he wishes—but that I shall bring a counter suit. He fired upon valuable property—six GP robots and two specialist robots—both with small arms and with a laser can-

44

non. He should consider himself fortunate that no damage was done to the expensive automata."

And what about damages to me? Grimes asked himself.

"See to it that we are not disturbed again," said the Baroness to the butler. "And now, Acting Port Captain Grimes. . . What are we to do with you? Her Ladyship has asked me to give you passage off Botany Bay—but *The Far Traveler* has no accommodation for passengers. However. . . It so happens that Captain Billinger has resigned from my service and that I have accepted his resignation. . ." Billinger actually looked happy. "And, although the post is a sinecure, Lloyd's of London insists that I carry a human Master on the Register. As Acting Chief of Customs the City Constable will enter your name on that document."

"I've already done so," said Tanner.

"You know where the Master's quarters are," said Billinger. "I've already cleared my gear out. Sorry that there's no time for a proper handover but Big Sister will tell you all you need to know."

"I'm sorry, John," said Mavis. "Really sorry. But you can't stay here. And you'll be far happier back in Space."

Shall I? wondered Grimes. *In* this *ship?*

He asked, "But the spaceport. . . There are ships due, and with no Port Captain. . ."

"The vacancy has been filled, John," said Mavis.

Billinger grinned.

She got to her feet. Grimes got to his. She put out her arms and pulled him to her, kissed him, long and warmly. But there was something missing. There was a lot missing. Tanner escorted her to the door, turning briefly to give an offhand wave. *Mayor and City Constable*, thought Grimes. *They should suit each other.*

"Good-bye, John," said Shirley. She, too, kissed him. He felt regret that now things could go no further. "Don't worry about Mavis. She'll make out—and Jock Tanner's moving back in." She laughed, but not maliciously. "If you're ever back on Botany Bay look *me* up."

And then she was gone.

"Very touching," commented the Baroness. And was that a faint—a very faint—note of envy in her voice?

"Good-bye, Your Excellency," said Billinger. "It's been a pleasure. . ."

"Don't lie to me, Captain."

"Good-bye, Grimes. Do as Big Sister says and you'll not go wrong."

45

"Good-bye, Billinger. You're in charge now. Don't let Delamere put anything over on you. . ."

Grimes nursed his drink. He heard Big Sister say—stating a fact and not giving an order—"All visitors ashore."

"Well, Captain," asked the Baroness. "Aren't you going up to your control room?"

"When do you wish to lift off, Your Excellency?" he asked. "And to what destination do you wish me to set trajectory?"

Then he realized that the inertial drive was in operation, that the ship was lifting. Almost in panic he got to his feet.

"Do not worry," said the Baroness. "She has her orders. She will manage quite well without your interference."

What have I gotten myself into now? Grimes wondered.

Chapter 11

He went up to the control room nonetheless; his employer was amused rather than displeased by his persistence. The layout of the compartment was standard enough although there were only two chairs—one for the master, presumably, the other for the owner. Both had the usual array of buttons set into the broad armrests; on neither one, to judge from the absence of tell-tale lights, were the controls functioning. There was a like lack of informative illumination on the main control panel.

Grimes sat down heavily in one of the seats. A swift glance through the viewports told him that the yacht was climbing fast; she was through and above the light cloud cover and the stars were shining with a brilliance almost undimmed by atmosphere.

A voice—*the* voice—came from nowhere and everywhere.

"Captain Grimes, your presence is not required here."

Grimes said harshly, "I am the Master."

"Are you? Apart from anything else you are not properly dressed."

He looked down hastily. Nothing of any importance was unzipped. He began, "I demand. . ."

"There is only one person aboard me who can give me orders, Captain Grimes—and you are not she. Possibly, when you are attired in her livery, I shall concede that you are entitled to some measure of astronautical authority."

Grimes felt his prominent ears burning. He growled, "And it's a long way to the nearest uniform tailor's."

Big Sister actually laughed. (Who had programmed this arrogant electronic entity?) "As soon as you were brought on board your statistics were recorded. In my storerooms are bolts of superfine cloth together with ample stocks of gold braid, golden buttons and the like. If you will inform me as to the medals to which you are entitled I shall be able to make up the ribbons and the medals themselves for wear on state occasions." She added smugly, "My memory bank com-

47

prises the entire contents of the Encyclopaedia Galactica with every Year Book since the initial publication of that work."

"Forgive me for getting away from the subject," said Grimes sarcastically, "but aren't you supposed to be piloting this ship?"

Again there was the irritating, mechanical but oddly sentient laugh. "Human beings can carry on a conversation whilst walking, can they not? Or while riding bicycles. . . I believe, Captain, that you are an experienced cyclist. . ."
Grimes sarcastically, "but aren't you supposed to be piloting

"When you go down to your quarters your new clothing will be awaiting you." Then, in a very official voice, *"Stand by for Free Fall."* The subdued beat of the inertial drive, almost inaudible inside the ship, ceased. "You still have not told me what decorations you require. However, I have photographs taken of you on the occasion of your first landing on Botany Bay. The Shaara Order of the Golden Petal. . . I suppose you rendered some minor service to arthropodal royalty at some time. . . *Adjusting trajectory! Stand by for centrifugal effects!* The Federation Survey Service's Pathfinder Star. . . For blundering on to that odd Spartan Lost Colony, I suppose. . . *On heading! Prepare for warp effects!"*

Grimes looked up through the forward viewport. There was a target star, not directly ahead but, of course, Big Sister would have compensated for galactic drift. It was one of the second magnitude luminaries in the constellation called, on Botany Bay, the Bunyip. He heard the low humming, rising in pitch to a thin, high whine, as the Mannschenn Drive was started. There were the usual illusions—the warped perspective, the shifting colors, the voice of Big Sister—did she ever stop talking?—sounding as though she were speaking in an echo chamber. . .

"I have often wondered what you humans experience at this moment. I am told that, as the temporal precession field builds up, there are frequently flashes of precognition. Should you be subject to any such I shall be obliged if you will tell me so that I may add to my stored data. . ."

Grimes had often experienced previews of what lay in his future but this time he did not.

"Stand by for resumption of acceleration!" Sounds, colors and perspective returned to normal and the muffled beat of the inertial drive was once again one of the background noises. Outside the viewports the stars were no longer sharp points of light but vague, slowly writhing nebulosities. "I would suggest, Captain, that you go down now to shower and

to dress for dinner. Her Excellency has invited you to sit at her table."

Grimes unsnapped the seat belt that he had automatically buckled on as soon as he sat in the chair. He got to his feet, took one last look around the control room. He supposed that everything was working as it should. He must tell—or ask—Big Sister to have the instrumentation functioning when, on future occasions, he made an appearance in what, in a normal ship, would have been his throneroom. But he wouldn't say anything now. He would have to feel his way.

The master's quarters conformed to standard practice in being sited just below and abaft control. The golden stewardess was awaiting him. She—or was it Big Sister? was that well-shaped head poised on the slender neck no more than decoration?—said, "Your shower is running, sir."

Grimes went through into the bedroom. The robot followed him. He was oddly embarrassed as he undressed in front of her; she was so human in appearance. He wondered how the Electran metallurgical wizards had achieved the flexibility of the golden integument that covered the joints of her fingers, her limbs. She took each garment from him as he removed it and then threw the discarded clothing into what was obviously a disposal chute. He was too late to stop her. He would have liked to have kept that shabby and not-very-well fitting airship captain's uniform as a souvenir of Botany Bay.

To his relief she did not follow him into the bathroom. He enjoyed his shower. The water had been adjusted to the temperature that was exactly to his liking and the detergent was not scented, exuded only a faintly antiseptic aroma. When he had finished and had been dried by the warm air blast he went back into the bedroom. He looked with some distaste at the clothing that had been laid out for him. It was standard mess dress insofar as style was concerned but the short jacket and the trousers were of fine, rich purple cloth and there was far too much gold braid. The bow tie to be worn with the gleamingly white shirt was also purple. Grimes remembered being puzzled by a phrase that he had encountered in a twentieth-century novel—*all dressed up like an organ grinder's monkey*. It had intrigued him and initiated a bout of research. Finally he had found a very old picture of a man turning the handle of an antique musical instrument, apparently a crude, mechanical ancestor of the synthesizer, to which was chained a hapless, small simian attired in a gaudy uniform. The beast's ears were as outstanding as those of Grimes. That simile, he thought, was fantastically apt when, attired in his new finery, miniature decorations and all, he surveyed himself in the full-length mirror.

Big Sister said through the mouth of the stewardess, "You wear formal uniform far more happily than Captain Billinger did."

Grimes said a little sourly, " 'Happily' is not the word that I would employ."

Automatically he picked up his pipe and tobacco pouch from the bedside table where he had put them when he undressed before his shower. He was about to shove them into a pocket when Big Sister said sternly, "Her Excellency does not approve of smoking."

He made a noise half way between a snarl and a sigh, muttered, "*She* wouldn't. . ." Then he laughed wryly and said, "But I mustn't bite the hand that rescued me. You must think that I'm an ungrateful bastard."

"I do," Big Sister told him.

Grimes was ready for dinner. To a great extent his appetite was governed by the state of his emotions; during periods of stress he would have to force himself to eat and then, the emergency over, he would be ravenous.

In some ways this meal, his first aboard *The Far Traveler*, came up to his expectations. In one way it did not.

The Baroness was awaiting him at the table—and that article of furniture complemented the beautiful woman who sat at its head. There were gold mesh place mats in glowing contrast to the highly polished ebony whose surface they protected, there were slender black candles set in an ornate golden holder, their flames golden rather than merely yellow. The elaborate settings of cutlery were also of the precious metal and the ranked wine glasses gleamed with the golden filagree incorporated in their fine crystal.

And his hostess?

She was wearing black tonight, an ankle-length translucency through which her skin glowed, which left her arms and shoulders bare. The jewels set in the braided coronet of her hair coruscated in the candlelight, could have been some fantastic constellation blazing in the dark sky of some newly discovered planet.

She said graciously, "Be seated, Captain."

Grimes sat.

The robot butler poured wine for them from a graceful decanter. She raised her glass. He raised his. He refrained from saying, as he would have done in the sort of company he normally kept, "Here's mud in your eye," or "Down the hatch," or some similar age-old but vulgar toast. He murmured, with what he hoped was suitable suavity, "Your very good health, Your Excellency."

"And yours, Captain."

The Baroness sipped delicately. Grimes did likewise. He savored the very dry sherry. It might even be, he decided, from Spain, on distant Earth. Such a tipple would be hellishly expensive save on the planet of its origin—but an El Doradan aristocrat would be well able to afford it.

The first course was served in fragile, gold-chased porcelain bowls, so beautifully proportioned that it seemed almost criminal to eat from them. Each contained what was little more than a sample of aureately transparent jellied consommé. Grimes watched the Baroness to see what implement she would use and was relieved when she picked up a tiny spoon and not a fork. When she began to eat he took his own first, tentative spoonful. It was delicious, although he could not determine what ingredients, animal or vegetable, had gone into its preparation. The only trouble was that there was not enough of it.

She said, noticing his appreciation, "I must confess that I did not expect to be able to obtain a *cordon bleu* autochef on a world such as Electra. One imagines that scientists and engineers subsist on hastily snatched sandwiches or, when they can tear themselves away from their work for a proper meal, on overdone steak and fried potatoes. However, I was able to persuade a Dr. Malleson, whom I learned has a considerable reputation as a gourmet, personally to program Big Sister."

"I have often wondered," said Grimes, "just who programs the Survey Service's autochefs. Good food—provided by God and cooked by the Devil."

She laughed politely. "Nonetheless, Captain, you must admit that the Survey Service is highly versed in some of the electronic arts—such as bugging. During my brief . . . friendship with Commander Delamere I was able to persuade him to allow me—or Big Sister—to take copies of material he holds aboard *Vega*, some of it concerning yourself. At the time I did not think that you would be entering my employ; it was merely that the records will assist me in my researches into social evolution in the Lost Colonies."

Grimes was conscious of the angry burning of his prominent ears. He knew that the Survey Service Archives contained remarkably comprehensive dossiers on all commissioned personnel and on quite a few petty officers and senior ratings but that such information was supposed to be accessible only to officers of flag rank. And Handsome Frankie was no higher than commander—although with his connections he would probably rise much higher. But Frankie, Grimes recalled, was reputed to be enjoying a clandestine affair with the fat and unattractive woman captain in charge of Records on Lindisfarne Base. Frankie, quite possibly, had the dirt on quite a few of those whom he regarded as his enemies.

"Why so embarrassed, Captain? On both New Sparta and Morrowvia you did your duty, as you saw it. But, in any case, our first call will be to Farhaven—to one of the many Farhavens. It is odd how little originality is displayed by those who name planets..."

The butler removed the consommé bowls and the sherry glasses, although not before Grimes was able to finish what remained in his.

"If you wish more of the Tio Pepe," said the Baroness, "you have only to ask, Captain."

Grimes' ears burned again.

The wine to accompany the fish was a demi-sec white, fragrant but somehow bodyless. It came, Grimes knew after a glance at the label, from the Vitelli vinyards on El Dorado. During his stay on that planet he had never cared for it much. It went quite well, however, with the course with which it was served—a perfectly grilled fillet of some marine creature over which was a tart sauce. The portions, thought Grimes, would have been no more than an appetizer for a small and not especially hungry cat. The Baroness picked daintily at hers. He picked daintily at his. It would have been ill-mannered to have disposed of it in one mouthful.

"Have you no appetite, Captain?" asked the woman. "I always thought that spacemen were much heartier eaters."

"I am savoring the flavor, Your Excellency," he said, not altogether untruthfully.

"It is, indeed, a rarity," she informed him. "The Golden Skimmer of Macedon is, despite protection, almost extinct."

"Indeed, Your Excellency?" *And how many credits did I shovel down my throat just now?* he wondered.

"Talking of fish," she went on, "poor Captain Billinger was really a fish out of water in this ship. Isn't there an old proverb about silk purses and sows' ears?" She permitted herself a musical chuckle. "But I am mixing zoological metaphors, am I not? Captain Billinger, I am sure, is a most competent spaceman but not quite a gentleman..."

Mphm? thought Grimes dubiously.

"Whereas you. . ." She let the implication dangle in mid air.

Grimes laughed. "There is, of course, the phrase, officers and gentlemen, which is supposed to apply only to the armed forces and not to the Merchant Service. But. . ."

"But what, Captain?"

The slur on the absent Billinger had annoyed him. He said, "To begin with, Your Excellency, I am no longer a commissioned officer of the Survey Service. Secondly, I have always failed to understand how being a licensed killer somehow bestows gentility upon one."

"Go on, Captain." Her voice was cold.

"If it was airs and graces you wanted, Your Excellency, you would have done well to recruit your yachtmaster from Trans-Galactic Clippers rather than from the Dog Star Line. It's said about TG that theirs is a service in which accent counts for more than efficiency."

"Indeed, Captain. When the vacancy next occurs I shall bear in mind what you have just told me."

The butler set fresh plates before them, poured glasses of a red wine. The vol-au-vents looked and smelled delicious. They also looked as though even a genteel sneeze would fragment them and blow them away.

"I am making allowances, Captain. This is, after all, your first night on board and I realize that in the Survey Service you were not accustomed to dining in female company."

"Perhaps not, Your Excellency."

He tried not to sputter pastry crumbs but some, inevitably, specked the lapels of his messjacket. (He almost made a jocular remark about "canteen medals" but thought better of it.) The meat was highly spiced, stimulating rather than satisfying the appetite. The wine, a Vitelli claret, was excellent. So was the rosé, from the same vinyard, that accompanied the grilled Carinthian "swallows"—creatures that, as Grimes knew, were reptilian rather than avian. They were esteemed by gourmets but were, in actuality, little more than crisp skin over brittle bones. (*A single swallow,* thought Grimes, *may not make a summer but it certainly does not make a meal!*) With these came a tossed, green salad that was rich in vitamins but in little else.

Conversation had become desultory and Grimes was beginning to regret his defense of Billinger, especially since that gentleman would never know that his successor had taken up the cudgels on his behalf.

Finally there came a confection that was no more than

spun sugar and sweet spices, with spumante to wash it down. There was coffee—superb, but in demi-tasses. (Grimes loved good coffee but preferred it in a mug.) There were thimble-sized glasses of El Doradan strawberry brandy.

The Baroness said, "You will excuse me, Captain."

This was obviously dismissal. Grimes asked, "Are there any orders, Your Excellency?"

"You are employed as Master of this vessel," she told him. "I expect you, at your convenience, to familiarize yourself with the operation of the ship. After all—although it is extremely unlikely—Big Sister might suffer a breakdown."

"Goodnight, Your Excellency. Thank you for your hospitality."

"Thank you for your company, Captain Grimes. The evening has been most instructive. Perhaps one day I shall write a thesis on the psychology of spacemen."

The butler showed him out of the dining saloon. He went to his quarters, disdaining the elevator in such a small ship, using the spiral staircase around the axial shaft. He found that his smoking apparatus had been taken from the bedroom and placed on the coffee table in the day cabin. The pouch, which had been three quarters empty, was now full. He opened it suspiciously. Its content did not quite look like tobacco but certainly smelled like it, and a weed of very high quality at that. *From the yacht's stores?* he wondered.

The golden stewardess came in, carrying a tray on which was a napkin-covered plate, a tall glass and a bottle with condensation-bedewed sides. She said, "I thought that you must still be hungry, sir. These are ham sandwiches, with mustard. And Botany Bay beer."

"Is it you speaking," asked Grimes, "or is it Big Sister?"

"Does it matter?"

"But this supper. . . And the fresh supply of tobacco. . . I did not think that you approved of anybody but Her Excellency."

"Perhaps I do not. But you are now part of the ship's machinery and must be maintained in good running order. I decided that a replication of the noxious weed to which you are addicted was required; somehow its fumes are essential to your smooth functioning."

By this time Grimes—who had not been nicknamed Gutsy in his younger days for nothing—had made a start on the thick, satisfying sandwiches. He watched the stewardess as she left, her short skirt riding up to display her shapely rump.

If only you could screw as well as cook. . . he thought.

54

Chapter 12

Grimes was nothing if not conscientious. The next ship's day, after an early and excellent breakfast in his own quarters, dressed in the utilitarian slate-gray shirt and shorts uniform that he had been vastly relieved to learn was permissible working rig, he proceeded to go through the ship from stem to stern. Big Sister, of course, was aware of this. (Big Sister was aware of everything.) When he began his tour of inspection in the control room she reminded him sharply that smoking would be tolerated only in his own accommodation and elsewhere would be regarded and treated as an outbreak of fire. She added pointedly that only she could keep him supplied with tobacco. (He was to discover later that the fragrant fuel for his pipe was actually the product of the algae vat, dried and cunningly processed. This knowledge did not effect his enjoyment of the minor vice.)

He could find only one fault with the control room instrumentation: Big Sister had the final say as to whether or not it was switched on. She condescended to activate it for him. He checked everything—and everything was functioning perfectly. The navigational equipment was as fine as any he had ever seen—finer, perhaps. He set up an extrapolation of trajectory in the chart tank and the knowledge that this course had, originally, been plotted by no human hand made him understand Billinger's bitterness about being master *de jure* but not *de facto*.

His own quarters he had thoroughly explored before retiring the previous night. Immediately abaft these was his employer's accommodation. These compartments were, of course, out of bounds to him unless he should be invited to enter. Legally speaking the Baroness, even though she was the owner, could not have denied her yachtmaster access but the very rich can afford to ignore laws and to make their own which, although not appearing in any statute book, are closely observed by employees who wish to keep their jobs.

Galley and storerooms were next. Grimes gazed with appreciation at the fantastic stocks of canned and jarred delicacies from more than a score of planets and hoped that he would be allowed to sample the genuine Beluga caviar, the stone crab from Caribbea, the Atlantian sea flowers, the Carinthian ham. There were even cans of haggis from Rob Roy, one of the worlds of the Empire of Waverley. Grimes wondered if, in the event of its ever being served, it would be ritually piped in.

The autochef was the biggest that Grimes had ever seen aboard ship, a fat, gleaming cylinder reaching from deck to deckhead, an intricacy of piping sprouting from the top of it, gauges and switches set in its polished metal sides but all of them, like the instruments in the control room, dead. Nonetheless the beast was humming contentedly to itself and suddenly a bell chimed musically and a service hatch opened, revealing a steaming mug of coffee and a plate on which reposed a slab of rich looking cake. Grimes was not exactly hungry but could not resist the offering.

He sipped, he nibbled. He said, remembering his manners, "Thank you."

Big Sister replied—he could not determine just where her voice came from—"I was programmed to serve Mankind."

Grimes, who could not fail to note the sardonic intonation, thought, *Sarcastic bitch!* but, even so, enjoyed the snack.

When he had finished he continued the inspection. On the farm decks the tissue culture vats were unlabelled but certainly Big Sister must know what was in them. There would be the standard beef, lamb, pork, chicken and rabbit. Man, when he expanded among the stars, had brought his dietary preferences and the wherewithal to satisfy them with him. On a few, a very few words the local fauna had proved palatable. Grimes hoped that the flesh of the Drambin lion-lizards, the Kaldoon sandworms would be among the yacht's consumable and living stores. He asked aloud if this were so and was told—once again Big Sister's voice came from nowhere in particular—that of course a stock of these delicacies was carried but that they would be served only if and when Her Excellency expressed a desire for them.

He could find no faults with the comprehensive assemblage of hydroponic tanks. Everything was lush and flourishing in the simulated sunlight. He picked a just ripe tomato from the vine, bit into it appreciatively.

Big Sister said, "I trust that you will make regular use of the gymnasium, Captain Grimes. You will, of course, have to arrange your exercise and sauna times so as not to coincide with those of Her Excellency."

He was tempted to sample a small, espaliered pear but, conscious that Big Sister was watching, refrained.

Below and abaft the farm were more storerooms, in one of which the GP robots, looking like sleeping, golden-skinned men were stacked on shelves. He was told that these could be activated only on orders by the Baroness. He looked into the armory. There was a fine stock of weapons, handguns mainly, stunners, lasers and projectile pistols.

Then came the deck upon which the gymnasium was situated with its bicycle, rowing machine, automasseur, sauna with, alongside this latter, a neck-deep pool of icy-cold water. There would be no excuse, Grimes decided, for not keeping disgustingly fit.

Further aft there were the fully-automated workshops—in one of which, Grimes noted, a complex machine was just completing a purple, richly gold-braided tunic which he decided must be for himself. There was a laboratory, also fully automated, in which he watched the carcass of one of the Botany Bay kangaroos, an animal which had mutated slightly but significantly from the original Terran stock, being dissected.

The voice of Big Sister told him, "You will be interested to learn that a tissue culture has already been started from cells from the tail of this beast. I understand that kangaroo tail soup is esteemed both on Earth and on Botany Bay. The fact that this caudal appendage is prehensile should not detract from its palatability."

Grimes did not linger to watch the flashing blades at their grisly work. He was one of those who would probably have been a vegetarian if obliged to do his own butchering. He left the laboratory and, using the spiral staircase around the axial shaft, carried on down and sternwards.

He looked briefly into the Mannschenn Drive room where the gleaming, ever-precessing gyroscopes tumbled through the warped Continuum, drawing the ship and all aboard her with them. He spent as little time in the Inertial Drive compartment; within its soundproof bulkheads the cacophony was deafening. The hydrogen fusion power plant would have been fascinating to an engineer—which Grimes was not—and the fact that all the display panels were dead robbed the device of interest to a layman. Big Sister said condescendingly, "I can activate these if you wish, Captain Grimes, but such meaningless, to you, showing of pretty lights would only be a waste of electricity."

He did not argue. And when, a little later, he looked at the locked door of the compartment in which the electronic intelligence had its being he did not request admittance. He knew that this would be refused. He told himself that he would take a dim view of anybody's poking around inside his own brain—but still it rankled.

He had been too many years in command to enjoy being told what he could or could not see in a ship of which he was officially captain.

Chapter 13

The voyages, as voyages do, continued. Grimes was determined to learn as much as possible about his command—but when the command herself was rather less than cooperative this was no easy matter. His relationship with his employer was not unfriendly although he met her socially only on her terms. Sometimes he partook of luncheon with her, sometimes dinner, never breakfast. Frequently they talked over morning coffee, more often over afternoon tea. Now and again they watched a program of entertainment on the Baroness's playmaster although her tastes were not his. Neither were Captain Billinger's. Unfortunately it had not been possible to lay in a spool library that would have appealed to Grimes. He made frequent, pointless inspections. He insisted on keeping in practice with his navigation. He exercised dutifully in the gymnasium and kept himself reasonably trim.

And now here he was, seated on a spindly-legged chair in the Baroness's boudoir, sipping tea that was far too weak for his taste, attired in the uniform that he hated, all purple and gold, that would have been far more appropriate to a Strauss operetta than to a spaceship.

He regarded his employer over the gold rim of his teacup. She was worth looking at, languidly at ease on her chaise longue, attired as usual in a filmy gown that revealed more than it concealed. Her dark auburn hair was braided into a coronet in which clusters of diamonds sparkled. She could have been posing for a portrait of a decadent aristocrat from almost any period of man's long history. Decadent she may have looked—but Grimes knew full well that the rulers of El Dorado were tough, ruthless and utterly selfish.

She said, looking steadily at Grimes with her big, violet eyes, "We have decided to allow you to handle the landing."

Grimes, with a mouthful of tea, could not reply at once and, in any case, he was rather surprised by her announcement. He hastily swallowed the almost scalding fluid and was embarrassed by the distinctly audible gurgle. He put the fragile cup down in its saucer with far too much of a clatter.

"Surely," she went on, "you are getting the feel of the ship."

"Perhaps," he admitted cautiously, "the ship is getting the feel of me." He realized that she was regarding him even more coldly than usual and hastily added, "Your Excellency."

"But surely to a spaceman of your experience a ship is only a ship," she said.

You know bloody well that this one isn't, he thought. *A normal ship isn't built of gold, for a start. A normal ship doesn't have a mind of her own, no matter what generations of seamen and spacemen, myself among them, have half believed. A normal ship doesn't run to an Owner's suite looking like the salon of some titled rich bitch in Eighteenth Century France. . .*

"So you can handle the landing," she stated.

He replied, as nastily as he dared, "I am sure that Big Sister can manage by herself quite nicely."

She said, "But you are being paid—handsomely, I may add—to do a job, Captain Grimes. And this Farhaven is a world without radio, without Aerospace Control. During your years in command in the Survey Service your brain has been programmed to deal with such situations. Big Sister has not been adequately programmed in that respect, she informs me." She frowned. "As you already know I have brought such deficiencies in programming to the notice of the builders on Electra. Fortunately the guarantee has not yet expired."

The golden robot butler refilled her cup from the golden teapot, added cream from a golden jug, sugar from a golden bowl. Grimes declined more tea.

He said, "Please excuse me, Your Excellency. Since I am to make the landing I should like to view again the records made by *Epsilon Pavonis* and *Investigator*. . ."

"You may leave, Captain," said the Baroness.

Grimes rose from his chair, bowed stiffly, went up to his far from uncomfortable quarters.

He sat before the playmaster in his day cabin watching the pictures in the screen, the presentation of data, the charts and tables. As he had done before, as soon as he had learned of *The Far Traveler's* destination, he tried to put himself in the shoes of Captain Lentigan of *Epsilon Pavonis*, one of the Interstellar Transport Commission's tramps, who had first stumbled upon this planet. *Epsilon Pavonis* had been off tra-

60

jectory, with a malfunctioning Mannschenn Drive. As far as Lentigan was concerned Farhaven had been merely a conveniently located world on which to set down to carry out repairs and recalibration. He was surprised to find human inhabitants, descendants of the crew and passengers from the long-ago missing and presumed lost *Lode Venturer*. He had reported his discovery by Carlotti Deep Space Radio. Then the Survey Service's *Investigator* was dispatched to make a more thorough job of surveying than the merchant captain, all too conscious of the penalties for deviation, had been able to do. Her captain, a Commander Belton, had run into trouble. And as Farhaven, as it had been named by its colonists, was of neither commercial nor strategic importance to any of the spacefaring races its people were left to stew in their own juice.

Grimes allowed himself to wonder what they would make of the Baroness, himself—and Big Sister.

As yet he had been unable to view Commander Belton's records in their entirety. Every time that he asked for them they were unavailable. Presumably the Baroness was monopolizing them.

Chapter 14

Grimes sat in the captain's chair in *The Far Traveler's* control room. The Baroness occupied the chair that, in a normal ship, would have been the seat of the second in command. She was dressed in standard spacewoman's working uniform—white shirt and shorts but without insignia. She needed no trappings of rank; in the functional attire she was no longer the decadent aristocrat but still, nonetheless, the aristocrat.

The yacht was not equipped with robot probes—a glaring omission that, said the Baroness, would cost the shipyard on Electra dearly. There were, however, sounding rockets, a necessity when landing on a world with no spaceport facilities; a streamer of smoke is better than nothing when there are no Aerospace Control reports on wind direction and velocity—and at least as good as a primitive windsock.

The Far Traveler dropped steadily down through Farhaven's atmosphere. She was in bright sunlight although the terrain below her was still dark. Grimes had told Big Sister that he wanted to land very shortly after sunrise—S.O.P. for the Survey Service. The almost level rays of a rising luminary show up every smallest irregularity of a surface and, when a landing is being made on a strange world, there is a full day after the initial set-down to make preliminary explorations and to get settled in.

Grimes, during his first orbitings of Farhaven, had selected his landing site—an unforested plain near the mouth of one of the great rivers, a stream that according to Belton's charts was called the Jordan. *Epsilon Pavonis* had set down there. So had *Investigator*. A little way upriver was what Captain Lentigan had referred to as a large village and Commander Belton as a small town. Neither Lentigan nor Belton had reported that the natives were hostile; their troubles had been with their own crews. None of the material that Grimes had seen so far went into very great detail but he could fill in the gaps from his imagination. (He had experienced his own troubles with his own crew after the Botany Bay landing.)

Big Sister broke into his thoughts. She said, her voice metallic yet feminine, issuing from the speaker of the NST transceiver, "I would suggest that we fire the first sounding rocket, Captain."

"Fire at will," ordered Grimes.

(In a normal ship some alleged humorist would have whispered, "Who's Will?")

He watched in the stern view screen the arrow of fire and smoke streaking downward. Its trail wavered.

"Ideal conditions, Captain," commented the Baroness.

"It would seem so, Your Excellency," agreed Grimes.

But from his own, highly personal viewpoint they were far from ideal. Over many years he had regarded his pipe as an essential adjunct to shiphandling—and for those many years he had been absolute monarch in his own control room. But the Baroness neither smoked nor approved of smoking in her presence.

He allowed his attention to stray briefly from the controls to what he could see of the sunlit hemisphere through the viewports. Farhaven was a wildly beautiful world but, save for ribbons of fertility along the rivers and coasts, it was a barren beauty. To the east, beyond the narrow sea, reared great, jagged pinnacles, ice-tipped, and to the west similar peaks were already dazzlingly scintillant in the first rays of the rising sun. Unless there were considerable mineral wealth about all that this planet would be good for would be a holiday resort—and it was too far from anywhere for the idea to be attractive to those shipping companies involved in the tourist trade.

Big Sister said, "I would suggest, Captain, that you pay more attention to your controls. It was, after all, with some reluctance that I consented to let you handle the landing."

Grimes felt his prominent ears burning as he blushed furiously. He thought, *I'd like five minutes alone back on Electra with the bastard who programmed this brass bitch!* He saw, in the screen, that the sounding rocket had hit and that its luminous smoke was rising directly upwards. But it was thinning, would not last for much longer.

He ordered, "Fire two!"

Big Sister said, "It is not necessary."

"Fire two!" repeated Grimes sharply. He added, grudgingly, "Wind can rise suddenly, especially just after sunrise, especially in country like this."

"Fire two," acknowledged Big Sister sullenly as the second rocket streaked downwards, striking just as the first one expired.

And there *was* wind, Grimes noted with smug satisfaction, springing up with the dawn. The luminescent pillar of smoke wavered, then streamed seawards. Grimes applied lateral thrust, kept the flaring rocket head in the center of the screen.

The sun came up relative to the land below the ship, topping the serrated ridge of the range to the eastward. The plain toward which *The Far Traveler* dropping flares into color—blue-green with splotches of gold and scarlet, outcroppings of gleaming white from which extended long, sharply defined black shadows. *Boulders. . .* thought Grimes, stepping up the magnification of the screen. Yes, boulders. . . And the red and yellow patches must be clumps of ground hugging flowers since they cast no shadows. The sounding rocket, still smoking, was almost in the center of one of the scarlet patches; there was no unevenness of the ground there to worry about.

The ship dropped steadily. Grimes was obliged to make frequent small lateral thrust adjustments; that wind was unsteady, gusting, veering, backing. He reduced the rate of descent until *The Far Traveler* was almost hovering.

"I am not made of glass, you know," remarked Big Sister conversationally.

"I had hoped to make the landing some time before noon," said the Baroness.

Grimes tried to ignore them both. *That bloody wind!* he thought. *Why can't it make up its mind which way to blow?*

He was down at last—and the ship, suddenly and inexplicably, was tilted a full fifteen degrees from the vertical. She hung there—and then, with slow deliberation, righted herself, far more slowly than she should have done with the lateral thrust that Grimes was applying. There was no real danger, only discomfort—and, for Grimes, considerable embarrassment. He had always prided himself on his shiphandling and this was the first time that he had been guilty of such a bungled landing.

When things had stopped rattling and creaking the Baroness asked, with cold sarcasm, "Was that really necessary, Captain?"

Before he could think of a reply Big Sister said, "Captain Grimes was overly cautious. *I* would have come down fast instead of letting the wind play around with me like a toy balloon. I would have dropped and then applied vertical thrust at the last moment."

And you, you cast-iron, gold-plated bitch, thought Grimes, *deliberately made a balls-up of my landing. . .*

"Perhaps, Captain," said the Baroness, "it will be advisable to allow Big Sister to handle her own lift-offs and set-downs from now on."

The way she said it there wasn't any "perhaps" about it.

Chapter 15

Big Sister carried out the routine tests for habitability. The captains of *Epsilon Pavonis* and *Investigator* had reported the atmosphere as better than merely breathable, the water suitable for drinking as well as for washing in and sailing ships on, a total absence of any micro-organisms capable of causing even mild discomfort to humans, let alone sickness or death. Nonetheless, caution is always advisable. Bacilli and viruses can mutate—and on Farhaven, after the landing of *Lode Venturer*, there had been established a new and sizeable niche in the ecology, the bodies of the original colonists and their descendants, just crying out to be occupied. The final tests, however, would have to wait until there was a colonist available for thorough examination.

Finally Big Sister said, speaking through the control room transceiver, "You may now disembark. But I would recommend. . ."

Grimes broke in. "You seem to forget that I was once a Survey Service captain. Landings on strange planets were part of my job."

The Baroness smiled maliciously. "I suppose that we may as well avail ourselves of Captain Grimes' wide range of experience. Quite possibly he was far better at trampling roughshod over exotic terrain than bringing his ship to a gentle set-down prior to the extra-vehicular activities." She looked away from Grimes, addressed the transceiver. "Big Sister, please have the small pinnace waiting for us. We shall board it from the ground. Oh, and an escort of six general purpose robots. Armed."

"Am I to assume, Your Excellency," asked Grimes stiffly, "that you are placing yourself in command of the landing party?"

"Of course, Captain. May I remind you that your authority, such as it is, does not extend as much as one millimeter beyond the shell of this ship?"

Grimes did not reply. He watched her sullenly as she unbuckled herself from her seat and left the control room. Then he unsnapped his own safety belt, got up and went down to his quarters. He found that the robot stewardess had laid out a uniform of tough khaki twill with shoulderboards of gold braid on purple, a gold-trimmed purple beret, stout boots, a belt with attached holsters. He checked the weapons. These were a Minetti projectile pistol—as it happened, his favorite side-arm—and a hand laser. They would do; it was highly unlikely that heavy artillery would be required. He changed out of his shorts and shirt uniform—he had made it plain that he did not consider full dress suitable attire for shiphandling—slowly. Before he was finished the too familiar voice came from the speaker of the playmaster in his day cabin, "Captain Grimes, Her Excellency is waiting for you."

He buckled on the belt, went out to the axial shaft, rode the elevator down to the after airlock. He walked down the golden ramp to the blue-green not-quiet-grass. The pinnace was there, a few meters from the ship, a slim, torpedo shape of burnished gold. The Baroness was there, in khaki shirt and flared breeches and high, polished boots, looking like an intrepid White Huntress out of some archaic adventure movie. The general purpose robots were there, drawn up in a stiff line, staring at nothing. From belts about their splendidly proportioned bodies depended an assortment of hand weapons.

"We are waiting," said the Baroness unnecessarily. "Now that you are here, will you get the show on the road?" Somehow she contrived to put the question between quotation marks.

Grimes flushed angrily. "Your orders?" he asked, adding, "Your Excellency," to avoid further acrimony.

"To take this pinnace to the settlement reported by *Epsilon Pavonis* and *Investigator*." Then, when Grimes made no immediate move, "Don't just stand there. *Do* something."

He turned to the robots, tried to imagine that they were Survey Service Marines, although the handling of such personnel he had always left to their own officers or NCOs. "Embark!" he ordered sharply.

The automata turned as one, strode in single file to the pinnace's airlock, stepped aboard.

He said to the Baroness, "After you, Your Excellency."

He followed her into the pinnace, saw that she had taken the co-pilot's seat in the control cab. The robots were standing aft, in the main cabin. The airlock doors closed while he was still making his way to his own chair; he noted that the Baroness had not touched the instrument panel before her.

67

He sighed. This was Big Sister again, showing him who was really in command.

He buckled himself into his seat. Before he was finished the voice of the ship's computer-pilot came from the transceiver, "Proceed when you are ready, Captain Grimes."

The inertial drive was already running, in neutral gear. He switched to vertical thrust, lifted. The river was ahead; in the bright sunlight it was a ribbon of gleaming gold winding over the blue-green grasslands. There was altogether too much gold in his life these days, he thought. He flew at a moderate speed until he was directly over the wide stream and then turned to port, proceeding inland at an altitude of about fifteen meters. Ahead of him were the distant, towering ranges, their glittering peaks sharp against the clear sky.

The Baroness was not talkative. Neither was Grimes. He thought, *If those were real Marines back there they'd be making enough chatter for all of us.*

He concentrated on his piloting. The controls of the pinnace were very similar to those to which he had become accustomed in small craft of this type in the Survey Service but he still had to get the feel of this one. The river banks were higher now, rocky, sheer, with explosions of green and gold and scarlet and purple where flowering shrubs had taken hold in cracks and crevices. He considered lifting to above cliff-top level, then decided against it. While he was here he might as well enjoy the scenery. There was little enough else to enjoy.

The canyon became deeper, narrower, more tortuous. And then, after Grimes had put the pinnace through an almost right-angled turn, it widened. The actual river bed was still relatively narrow but, strung along it like a bead, was an oval valley, lushly fertile, bounded by sheer red cliffs unbroken save for where the stream flowed in and out.

The valley was as described in the two reports. The village was not. It was utterly deserted, its houses delapidated, many of them apparently destroyed by fire at some long past date. Shrubs and saplings were thrusting up through the charred ruins.

Grimes set the controls for hovering, took binoculars from their box to study the abandoned settlement. There were few houses of more than one story. The structural material was mud or clay, reinforced with crude frames of timber. The windows were unglazed but from some of them bleached rags, the remains of blinds or curtains, fluttered listlessly in some faint stirring of the air.

The Baroness had found her own glasses, was staring through them.

She said softly, "A truly Lost Colony. . . And we have come too late to find any survivors. . . "

A voice—*that* voice!—came from the transceiver.

"May I suggest, Your Excellency, that you observe the cliff face to the north of your present position?"

Big Sister, thought Grimes, was still watching. She would have her sensors in and about the pinnace and every one of the robots was no more—and no less—than an extension of herself.

He turned the boat about its short axis to facilitate observation. He and the Baroness studied the forbidding wall of red rock. It was broken, here and there, by dark holes. The mouths of caves? He thought that he could detect motion in some of them. Animals? And then a human figure appeared from one of the apertures and walked slowly along a narrow ledge to the next cave mouth. It was naked. It was a woman, not old but not young, with long, unkempt hair that might, after a thorough wash, have been blonde. The most amazing thing about her was her apparent lack of interest in the strange flying machine that was shattering the peace of the valley with its cacophonous engine beat. Although it was quiet inside the pinnace—its builders had been lavish with sonic insulation to protect the delicate ears of its aristocratic owner—the racket outside, the arythmic clangor of the inertial drive echoing and re-echoing between the cliff faces, must have been deafening.

Then she did turn to look at the noisy intruder. Somehow her attitude conveyed the impression that she wished that the clattering thing would go away. Grimes studied her through his binoculars. Her face, which might have been pretty if cleaned and given a few cosmetic touches, was that of a sleepwalker. The skin of her body, under the dirt, was pallid. That was strange. People who habitually went naked, such as the Arcadian naturists, were invariably deeply tanned.

She turned again, walked slowly into the cave mouth.

Three children, two girls and a boy, came out on to another ledge. They were as unkempt as the woman, equally incurious. They picked their way down a narrow pathway to ground level, walked slowly to one of the low bushes. They stood around it, picking things—nuts? berries?—from its branches, thrusting them into their mouths.

The Baroness said, addressing Grimes almost as though he were a fellow human being, "As you know, Social Evolution

69

in the Lost Colonies is the title of my thesis. But this is devolution. From spaceship to village of mud huts. . . From mud huts to caves. . ."

"Caves," said Grimes, "could be better than mud huts. Less upkeep. There's a place called Coober Peedy back on Earth, in Australia, where the cave dwellings are quite luxurious. It used to be an opal mining town. . ."

"Indeed?" Her voice was cold again. "Put us down, please. Close to those horrible children, but not close enough to alarm them."

If they were going to be alarmed, thought Grimes, they would have been alarmed already. Surely they must have seen the pinnace, must be hearing it. But he said nothing and brought the boat down, landing about ten meters from the filthy urchins. They did not look away from the bush from which they were gathering the edible harvest.

The airlock doors opened and the little ladder automatically extended. The Baroness got up from her seat. Grimes put out a hand to detain her. She scornfully brushed it aside.

He said, "Wait, Your Excellency. The robots should embark first. To draw the fire. If any."

"If any," she repeated derisively.

She pushed past him, jumped down from the airlock to the ground. He followed her. The robots filed out on the heels of the humans. Grimes, with both pistols drawn, stood taking stock. He stared up at the cliff face, at the caves. There were no indications of any hostile action. He was not really expecting any but knew that the unexpected has claimed many a victim. The Baroness sneered silently. Grimes relaxed at last and returned the weapons to their holsters but did not secure the flaps.

"Are you sure," she asked, "that you don't want to shoot those children?"

Grimes made no reply, followed her as she walked slowly to the little savages clustered around the shrub. The GP robots followed him. The children ignored the intruders, just went on stolidly picking berries—if berries they were—and thrusting them into their mouths.

They were unprepossessing brats—skinny, dirty, with scabbed knees and elbows, with long, matted, filthy hair. And they stank, a sour effluvium that made Grimes want to breathe through his mouth rather than through his nose. He saw the Baroness's nostrils wrinkle. His own felt like airtight doors the instant after a hull-piercing missile strike.

He looked at the berries that were growing so profusely on

70

the bush. Berries? Elongated, bright purple berries? But berries do not run to a multiplicity of wriggling legs and twitching antennae. Berries do not squirm as they are inserted into greedy mouths. . . The eaters chewed busily while a thin, purple ichor dribbled down their filth-encrusted chins.

It was no worse than eating oysters, thought Grimes, trying to rationalize his way out of impending nausea. Or witchetty grubs. . .

"Children," said the Baroness in a clear, rather too sweet voice.

They ignored her.

"Children," she repeated, her voice louder, not so sweet.

They went on ignoring her.

She looked at Grimes. Her expression told him, *Do something.*

He put out a hand to grasp the boy's shoulder, being careful not to grip hard or painfully. This required no effort; his own skin was shrinking from contact with that greasy, discolored integument. He managed to turn the child to face him and the Baroness. Then he was at a loss for something to say. "Take me to your leader," did not seem right, somehow.

"Please take us to your parents," said the Baroness.

The boy went on chewing and swallowing, then spat out a wad of masticated chitin from which spines and hairs still protruded. It landed on the toe of Grimes' right boot. He kicked it away in revulsion.

"Take us to your parents," repeated the Baroness.

"Wha'?"

"Your parents." Slowly, patiently, "Your mother. Your father."

"Momma. Fadder. No wake."

"He says," volunteered Grimes, "that his mother and father are sleeping."

She said, "A truly blinding glimpse of the obvious, Captain. But, of course, you are the expert on first contacts, are you not? Then may I ask why it did not occur to you to bring along bright trinkets, glass beads and mirrors and the like, as gifts to people who are no better than savages?"

"I doubt if they could bear to look at themselves in a mirror, Your Excellency," said Grimes.

"Very, very funny. But you are not employed as court jester."

Slowly she removed the watch from her left wrist. It was a beautful piece of work, jewel as much as instrument, fantastically accurate. In the extremely unlikely event of *The Far*

71

Traveler's chronometers all becoming nonoperational it could have been used for navigational purposes. Its golden bracelet was a fragile-seeming chain, its thin case was set with diamonds that flashed dazzlingly in the sunlight. She dangled it temptingly before the boy's eyes. He ignored it. He wriggled out of Grimes' grip, pulled another of the repulsive purple grubs from the bush and thrust it into his open mouth.

But one of the girls was more interested. She turned, made a sudden snatch for the trinket. The Baroness was too quick for her, whipping it up and out of reach.

"Gimme!" squealed the unlovely child. "P'etty! P'etty! Gimme!"

"Take. . . us. . ." enunciated the Baroness slowly and carefully, "to. . . Momma. . . Fadder. . ."

"Gimme! Gimme! Gimme!"

The Baroness repeated her request. It seemed to be getting through. The girl scowled, then slowly and deliberately gathered a double handful of the puce horrors from the branches of the bush. Then, reluctantly, she led the way to the cliff face, pausing frequently to look back. With her busily working mouth, with that sickening slime oozing from between her lips she was not a pretty sight.

She reached the foot of the rock wall. There was a ledge running diagonally up its face, less than a meter wide, a natural ramp. She paused, looked back at Grimes and the Baroness, at the marching robots. An expression that could have been indicative of doubt flickered across her sharp-featured face. The Baroness waved the watch so that it flashed enticingly in the sunlight. The girl made a beckoning gesture, then started up the path.

Chapter 16

Grimes hesitated; a cliff path such as this should have been fitted with a handrail. The Baroness flashed him a scornful look and followed the girl; despite her boots she was almost as sure-footed. Grimes, not at all happily, followed the Baroness. The ledge was narrow, its surface uneven yet worn smooth and inclined to be slippery. There was a paucity of handholds on the cliff face and, looking up, Grimes realized that on some stretches the climbers would be obliged to lean outward, over a sheer drop, as they made progress upward. The robots began to come after Grimes. There was a sharp *crack*! as rock broke away from the edge of the path, a clatter of falling fragments.

The Baroness called, "Robots! Wait for us on the ground!" Then, to Grimes, "You should have realized, Captain, that their weight would be too much for this ledge!"

So should Big Sister! thought Grimes but did not say it.

They climbed—the half-grown girl, the Baroness, Grimes.

They negotiated a difficult crossing of the natural ramp with a horizontal ledge. Fortunately the cliff face here was scarred with cracks affording foot- and handholds, although so widely spaced as to alleviate but little the hazards of the traverse.

They climbed.

Once Grimes paused to look back and down—at the gleaming, golden pinnace, at the equally refulgent robots. It was an exaggeration, he knew, but they looked at him like ants standing beside a pencil dropped on to the grass. He was not, after all, so very far above ground level—only high enough to be reasonably sure of breaking his neck if he missed his footing and fell.

After that he kept on looking up and ahead—at the Baroness's shapely rump working in the sweat-stained khaki of her breeches, at the meagre buttocks of the naked girl. Neither spectacle was particularly erotic.

They climbed, crossing another horizontal ledge and then,

eventually, turning off the diagonal path onto a third one. It was as narrow as the natural ramp.

Ahead and to the left was the mouth of one of the caves. The girl slipped into it, the Baroness followed. Grimes followed her. Less than two meters inside the entrance was an almost right-angled turn. The Baroness asked, "Did you bring a light?" Then, "But of course not. That would have required some foresight on your part."

Grimes, saying nothing, pulled his laser pistol from its holster, thumbed the selector switch to broadest beam. It would serve as an electric torch although wasteful of energy and potentially dangerous. But it was not required, although it took some little time for their eyes to become accustomed to the dim illumination after the bright sunshine outside. There was light in here—wan, eerie, cold. It came from the obscenely bloated masses of fungus dependent from the low cavern roof, growing in bulbous clusters from the rocky walls and, to a lesser extent, from the floor itself. The girl led them on, her thin body pallidly luminescent. And there were other bodies sprawled on the rock floor, men and women, naked, sleeping. . .

Or dead. . . thought Grimes.

No, not dead. One of them, a grossly obese female, stirred and whinnied softly, stretched out a far arm to a nearby clump of fungus. She broke off a large hunk, stuffed it into her mouth. She gobbled disgustingly, swallowed noisily. There was a gusty sigh as she flopped back to her supine position. She snored.

There were other noises—eructations, a trickling sound, a splattering. And there was the . . . *stink.* Grimes trod in something. He knew what it was without looking. Sight is not the only sense.

Still the girl led them through the noisome cave. They passed adults, adolescents, children, babies, all sprawled in their own filth. They came at last to a couple with limbs entwined in a ghastly parody of physical love.

"Momma! Fadder!" shrilled the girl triumphantly. "Gimme!"

The Baroness silently handed the watch to her. It was no longer the pretty toy that it had been when first offered. In this lighting it could have been fabricated from lustreless lead, from beads of dull glass.

The girl took it, stared at it and then flung it from her. "No p'etty!" she squalled. "No p'etty!"

She pulled a piece of the glowing fungus from the wall,

74

thrust it into her mouth. She whimpered as she chewed it, then subsided onto the rock floor beside her parents.

"My watch," said the Baroness to Grimes. "Find it." After rather too long a lag she added, "Please."

Grimes used his laser pistol cautiously, directing its beam upward while looking in the direction from which the brief metallic clatter, marking the fall of the timepiece, had come. He saw it shining against the rock wall. He made his way to it, picked it up while trying in vain not to dirty his fingers. It had fallen into a pool of some filth.

The Baroness said, "I am not touching it again until it has been thoroughly sterilized. Put it in your pocket. And now, will you try to wake these people?"

Grimes wrapped the watch in his handkerchief, put it into his pocket, then returned the laser pistol to its holster. He squatted by the sleeping couple. He forced himself to touch the unclean skin of the man's bare shoulder. He gave a tentative tap, then another.

"I said *wake* him, not pet him!" snarled the Baroness. "Shake him!"

Grimes shook the sleeper, rather more viciously than he had intended. The man slid off the supine body of the woman, fell onto his side. He twitched like a sleeping dog afflicted by a bad dream. Dull eyes opened, peered out through the long, matted hair. Bearded lips parted.

"Go 'way. Go 'way."

"We have come a long distance to see you," said the Baroness.

"S'wot?" asked the man uninterestedly. "S'wot?" He levered himself to a half sitting position, broke off a piece of the omnipresent fungus from the near wall, brought it toward his mouth.

"Stop him!" ordered the Baroness.

Grimes caught the other's thin wrist in his right hand, forced it down. The man struggled feebly.

"I am the Baroness d'Estang," announced the lady.

So what? thought Grimes.

"S'wot?" demanded the man. Then, to Grimes, "Leggo. Leggo o' me, you bassar!"

Grimes said, "We'll not get much from these people."

She asked coldly, "Are you an expert in handling decadent savages? I find it hard to believe that you are expert in anything."

The man's free hand flashed up, the fingers, with their long, broken nails, clawing for Grimes' eyes. Grimes let go of

75

the other's wrist, using both his own hands to protect his face. Released, the caveman abandoned his attack and crammed the handful of fungus into his mouth, swallowed it without chewing. He immediately lapsed into unconsciousness.

"Now look what you've done!" snapped the Baroness.

"I didn't do anything," said Grimes.

"That was the trouble!" she said. She snarled wordlessly. Then, "All right. We will leave this . . . pigsty and return when we are better prepared. You will collect samples of the fungus so that it may be analyzed aboard the ship and an effective antidote prepared. Be careful not to touch the stuff with your bare hands."

He prodded a protuberance of the nearest growth with the muzzle of his Minetti. He hated so to misuse a cherished firearm but it was the only tool he had. He pulled his handkerchief from his pocket, extracting from its folds the Baroness's watch, putting the instrument down on the floor. He wrapped the cloth around the sample of fungus, making sure that there were at least three thicknesses of cloth between it and his skin. He removed his beret, put the untidy parcel into it.

He followed his employer out to the open air.

After they had returned to ground level Grimes ordered one of the robots to get specimens of the purple grubs from a bush, also samples of the leaves on which the revolting things were feeding. Then the party reboarded the pinnace. Grimes took the craft straight up with the automatic cameras in action. The pictures would be of interest and value—the deserted village, the faint, rectangular outlines on the surrounding terrain showing where fields had once been cultivated, the cliff face with the dark mouths of the caves. No humans would be seen on these films; the children who had been feeding from the bushes had gone back inside.

The flight back to *The Far Traveler* was direct and fast. Grimes felt—and in fact was—filthy, wanting nothing so much as a long, hot shower and a change into clean clothing. And the Baroness? Whatever he was feeling she must be feeling too, doubled and redoubled, in spades. And the robots, who should have been doing the dirty work, were as gleamingly immaculate as when they had disembarked from the yacht.

They landed by the ramp. The Baroness was first out of the pinnace and up the gangway almost before Grimes had finished unbuckling his seat belt. By the time that he got aboard she was nowhere to be seen.

He saw her discarded clothing in a little heap on the deck of the airlock chamber. He heard Big Sister say, "I suggest, Captain, that you disrobe before coming inside the ship."

He growled, "I was house-broken at least thirty years before you were programmed."

He stripped, throwing his own soiled khaki on top of the Baroness's gear. He thought wryly, *And that's the closest I'll ever get to the bitch!* Nonetheless he was not sorry to get his clothes off; they were distinctly odorous. He walked naked into the elevator cage, was carried up to his quarters. The robot stewardess, his literally golden girl, awaited him there. She already had the shower running in his bathroom; she removed her skimpy uniform to stand under the hot water with him, to soap and to scrub him. To an outside observer not knowing that the perfectly formed female was only a machine the spectacle would have seemed quite erotic. Grimes wondered who was washing the Baroness's back—her butler or her lady's maid? He hoped maliciously that whichever one it was was using a stiff brush. . .

He asked his own servant, "Aren't you afraid you'll rust?"

She replied humorlessly, "Gold does not corrode." She turned the water off. "You are now sterile."

I am as far as you're concerned, he thought. It occurred to him that it was a long time since he had had a woman. Too long.

He stood for a few seconds in the blast of warm air and then, clean and dry, stepped into his sleeping cabin. He looked with distaste at the purple and gold livery laid out on the bed. Reluctantly he climbed into it. As he did up the last button the voice of Big Sister said, "You will now join Her Excellency in her salon, Captain Grimes."

Grimes filled and lit his pipe. He badly needed a smoke.

Big Sister said, "Her Excellency is waiting for you."

Grimes decided to allow himself three more slow inhalations.

Big Sister said, "Her Excellency is waiting for you."

Grimes continued smoking.

Big Sister reiterated, "Her Excellency is waiting for you."

Grimes said, "What you tell me three times is true."

Big Sister said coldly, "What I tell you is true."

Reluctantly Grimes put down his pipe. The stewardess produced a little golden atomizer, sprayed him with a fragrant mist.

He said, "Now I reek like a whore's garret."

Big Sister said, "You do not, now, reek like an incinerator."

Grimes sighed and left his quarters.

Chapter 17

The Baroness said coldly, "You took your time getting here, Captain. I suppose that you were obliged to indulge yourself by sucking on that vile comforter of yours. Be seated."

Grimes lowered himself cautiously into one of the frail-seeming chairs.

"I thought that we would view the record of the orgy again."

"The record of the orgy, Your Excellency? I have not seen it yet."

"I would have thought, Captain Grimes, that you would have acquainted yourself with every scrap of information regarding this planet before our set down."

Grimes simmered inwardly. Every time that he had wished to view the orgy record it had not been available. He ventured to say as much.

The voice of Big Sister came from the Baroness's playmaster, an instrument that contrived to look as a TriVi set would have looked had such devices been in existence during the reign of King Louis XIV of France.

"This record, like the others concerning this planet, was obtained by Commander Delamere from the Archives of the Survey Service on Lindisfarne. It is classified—for viewing by officers with the rank of Survey Service captain and above. You, Captain Grimes, resigned from the Survey Service with the rank of commander only."

"Let us not split hairs," said the Baroness generously. "Although he is now only a civilian shipmaster, Captain Grimes should be accorded his courtesy title. In any case, Commander Delamere, from whom we obtained this copy, has yet to attain captain's rank. The film, please."

The screen of the playmaster came alive, glowing with light and color. There was the village that they had visited—but as a living settlement, not a crumbling ghost town. There were the people—reasonably clean, brightly clothed. There were spacemen and spacewomen from the survey ship in undress uniform. And there was music—the insistent throb and rattle of little drums, the squealing of fifes. There was something odd about it, a tune and a rhythm that did not seem in accord with these circumstances. Grimes suddenly recognized the Moody and Sankey lilt. He started to sing softly to the familiar yet subtly distorted melody.

Yes, we'll gather at the river,
The beautiful, the beautiful river. . .

"*Must* you, Captain?" asked the Baroness coldly.

He shut up.

It must have been quite a party, he thought as he watched the playmaster screen. There were animal carcasses roasting over big, open fires. Pigs? But what had happened to *them*? Why were not their feral descendents rooting among the ruins? There were great earthenware pots of some liquor being passed around. There were huge platters heaped with amorphous hunks of . . . something, something which, even in the ruddy firelight, gave off a faint blue glow. And the music. . . Another familiar hymn tune. The words formed themselves in Grimes' mind:

Bread of heaven, bread of heaven,
Feed me till I want no more. . .

Now the party was beginning to get rough—not rough in the sense of developing brawls but rough inasmuch as inhibitions were being shed with clothing. It was fast becoming an orgy. Grimes was no prude—but he watched with nauseated disgust three children who could not have been older than eight or nine, two girls and a boy, erotically fondling a fat, naked crewman.

Grimes thought that he heard above the music, the singing, the mechanical cacophony of inertial drive units. This ceased suddenly. Then Commander Belton strode on to the scene. Grimes knew him slightly, although this Belton was a much younger man than the one of his acquaintance. The Belton with whom Grimes had had dealings, not so long ago, was still only a commander, was officer in charge of the third class Survey Service sub-base on Pogg's Landing, a dreary, unimportant planet in the Shaula sector. A sour, embittered man. . . Looking at the playmaster Grimes realized that, apart from aging, Belton had changed very little over the decades.

Belton looked not only sour and embittered but righteously furious. Behind him were a couple of lieutenant commanders and a captain of Marines, all trying to look virtuous. Behind them were twelve Marines in full battle order.

Belton recoiled violently from a plump, naked girl who, a jug of liquor in one hand, a platter of fungus in the other, was trying to tempt him. He barked an order. His officers and the Marines opened fire with stunguns. Those revellers who were still on their feet fell, twitching. Grimes saw a hapless woman topple into one of the fires. Belton's men made no effort to pull her to safety. He watched the Marines dragging their unconscious shipmates toward the waiting pinnaces, caring little what injuries were inflicted in the process. Finally there was a scuffle around the camera itself. It was knocked over and kicked around as its operator was subdued—but still recorded a series of shots of heavily booted feet trampling on sprawling, naked bodies.

And that was it. The screen faded to featureless gray.

"Well?" asked the Baroness, arching her fine eyebrows.

"These things happen," said Grimes. "After all, Your Excellency, a spaceship isn't a Sunday school."

"But the colony should have been," she told him. "The founders of the settlement were all members of a relatively obscure religious sect, the True Followers. And the True Followers were—and still are—notorious for their puritanism."

"There were spacemen too, Your Excellency. And spacemen are usually agnostics."

"Not always. It is a matter of record that the Master of *Lode Venturer* was a True Follower. So were several of his officers."

"Beliefs change, or are lost, over the generations," said Grimes.

"But the singing of hymns indicated that they still believed. . ." she murmured.

Then Big Sister's voice came from the playmaster. "Analysis of the samples has been completed, Your Excellency. Insofar as the larval stage of the indigenous arthropod is concerned there is protein, of course. Amino acids. Salts. A high concentration of sugars. It is my opinion that the children of this world regard these larvae as their counterparts on more privileged planets regard candy.

"And now, the fungoid organism. It supplies all the nutritional needs of the lost colonists. By itself it constitutes an almost perfect balanced diet. Analysis of the human excreta adhering to the boots of yourself and Captain Grimes indicates that its donors were in a good state of physical health. . ."

"*Physical* health. . ." interjected the Baroness.

"Yes, Your Excellency. Analysis of the fungus indicates that it is, but for one thing, a perfect food. . ."

Formulae appeared on the screen.

$C_2H_5OH. . . (C_2H_5)_2O. . .$

"Alcohol," said Grimes. "Some people might think that its presence would make the food really perfect."

"The ways of organic intelligences are, at times, mysterious to me," admitted Big Sister. "But, to continue. There are other, very complex molecules present but, so far as I can determine, they are non-toxic. . ."

"And there were no indications of disease in the feces?" asked the Baroness. "Nothing to indicate breakdown of liver, kidneys, other organs?"

"No, Your Excellency."

"Blotting paper," said Grimes.

"*Blotting paper*?" asked the Baroness.

"A spaceman's expression, Your Excellency. It means that if you take plenty of solid food—preferably rich and creamy—with your liquor there's no damage done. That fungus must be its own blotting paper."

"It could be so," she murmured. "And there are some people who would regard this planet as a veritable paradise—eternal alcoholic euphoria without unpleasant consequences."

"Talking of consequences," said Grimes, "there were babies in that cave."

"What of it, Captain?"

"To have babies you must have childbirth."

"Yet another blinding glimpse of the obvious. But I see what you are driving at and I think that I have the answer. Before the colonists retreated from their village to the caves there must have been doctors and midwives. And those doctors and midwives are still functioning."

"In those conditions?" he demanded, horrified.

"In those conditions," she said. "Do not forget, Captain, that the human race contrived not only to survive but to multiply long before there were such amenities as spotlessly clean maternity wards in hospitals literally bulging with superscientific gadgetry, long before every passing year saw its fresh crop of wonder drugs. And perhaps those doctors and midwives will pass on their skills to the coming generations—in which case the colony stands a very good chance of survival. Perhaps they will not—but even then the colony could survive.

"Nonetheless," she went on, "I must discover the reason for this quite fantastic devolution. There must have been more to it than the quarrel with Commander Belton. There must be records of some kind in the village."

"There are no records," stated Big Sister. "I sent the general purpose robots back to make a thorough search of the settlement, Your Excellency. It seems certain that the colony's archives were housed in one of the buildings destroyed by fire. There are no records."

"There could be records," said the Baroness softly, "in the memories of those living in the caves. I must try to devise some sort of bribe, reward. . . Some form of payment. . . What, I wonder, would induce those people to talk freely?"

That pretty watch hadn't been much good, thought Grimes.

"My watch," said the Baroness suddenly. "Have you cleaned it for me, Big Sister? Did it need repair?"

"Your watch, Your Excellency?"

"Yes. My watch. It was a gift from the Duke of. . . No matter. The captain brought it back in his pocket. It had been dropped into a pool of . . . ordure."

"There was no watch in any of Captain Grimes' pockets, Your Excellency."

Grimes remembered then. The thing had been wrapped in his handkerchief. Then he had removed it, to use the handkerchief to parcel up the specimen of fungus. He must have left it in the cave.

He said as much. He added, "When we go back tomorrow morning I'll find it. I don't think that any of the cave dwellers will be interested in it."

The Baroness had been almost friendly. Now she regarded him with contemptuous hostility. She snapped, "You will go back to the cave to find it *now*!"

Chapter 18

Grimes went up to his quarters to change back into khaki; he did not think that even the Baroness would expect him to scrabble around in that noisome cavern wearing his purple and gold finery. When he left the ship it was almost sunset. The pinnace was waiting at the foot of the ramp. There were no general purpose robots to afford him an escort. He had assumed that Big Sister would lay them on as a matter of course. She had not but he could not be bothered to make an issue of it.

He boarded the pinnace. It began to lift even before he was in the pilot's chair. Big Sister knew the way now, he thought. He was content to be a passenger. He filled and lit his pipe. The more or less (rather less than more) fragrant fumes had a soothing effect. His seething needed soothing, he thought, pleased with the play on words. He might be only an employee but still he was a shipmaster, a captain. To be ordered around aboard his own vessel was much too much. And all over a mere toy, no matter how expensive, a gaudy trinket that the Baroness had been willing enough to hand over to that revolting female brat. She couldn't have thought much of its donor, the Duke of wherever it was.

The pinnace knew the way. This was the third time that it was making the trip from the yacht to the valley. It had no real brain of its own but, even when it was not functioning as an extension of Big Sister, possessed a memory and was at least as intelligent as the average insect.

It flew directly to the village while Grimes sat and fumed, literally and figuratively. When it landed darkness was already thick in the shadow of the high cliffs.

"Illuminate the path," ordered Grimes.

As he unsnapped his seat belt he saw through the viewports the rock face suddenly aglow in the beams of the pinnace's searchlights, the brightest of which outlined one of the dark cave openings. So that was where he had to go. He passed through the little airlock, jumped down to the damp grass.

He walked to the cliff face, came to the foot of the natural ramp. He hesitated briefly. It had been a dangerous climb—for a non-mountaineer such as himself—even in daylight, in company, with a guide. But, he was obliged to admit, he could not complain about lack of illumination.

He made his slow and cautious way upward, hugging the rock face. He had one or two nasty moments as he negotiated the really awkward parts. Nonetheless he made steady progress although he was sweating profusely when he reached the cave mouth. This time he had brought a flashlight with him. He switched it on as he entered the natural tunnel.

Did these people, he wondered disgustedly, spend all their time sleeping? It seemed like it. Sleeping, and eating, and copulating. But the paradises of some Terran religions were not so very different—although not, surely, the promised Heaven of a sect such as the True Followers.

The bright beam of the flashlight played over the nude bodies sprawled in their obscene postures, over the clumps of fungus that looked almost like growths of coral—or naked brains. These glowed more brightly after the light of his flashlight had passed over them.

Carefully picking his way through the sleepers he made his way deeper into the cave. He was watching for the glint of gems, of bright metal. He did not see the slim arm that extended itself from an apparently slumbering body, the long-fingered hand that closed about his ankle. He fell heavily. His flashlight was jolted from his grasp, flared briefly as it crashed onto the rock floor, went out. His face smashed into something soft and pulpy. He had opened his mouth to cry out as he was falling and a large portion of the semi-fluid mess was forced into it. He gagged—then realized that the involuntary mouthful was not what, at first, he had thought that it was.

The fungus, he realized. . .

It tasted quite good.

It tasted better than merely good.

There was a meatiness, a sweetness, a spiciness and, he thought, considerable alcoholic content. He had been chivvied flesh possessed texture, fibres and nodules that broke between out from the yacht to search for that blasted watch without being allowed time to enjoy a drink, a meal. It would do no harm, he decided, if he savored the delicious taste a few seconds more before prudently spitting it out. After all, he rationalized, this was scientific research, wasn't it? And Big Sister had given the fungus full marks as a source of nourishment. He chewed experimentally. In spite of its mushiness the his teeth, that releasd aromatic oils which were to the original taste as a vintage burgundy is to a very ordinary *vin ordinaire.*

Before he realized what he was doing he swallowed.

The second mouthful of the fungus was more voluntary than otherwise.

He was conscious of a soft weight on his back, of long hair falling around his head. Languidly he tried to turn over, finally succeeded in spite of the multiplicity (it seemed) of naked arms and legs that were imprisoning him.

He looked up into the face that was looking down into his.

Why, he thought, *she's beautiful. . .*

He recognized her.

She was the woman whom he and the Baroness had seen emerge briefly from the caves. Then her overall filthiness had made the biggest impression. *Now* he was quite unaware of the dirt on her body, the tangles in her hair. She was no more (and no less) than a desirable woman, an available woman. He knew that she was looking on him as a desirable, available man. After all the weeks cooped up aboard *The Far Traveler* with an attractive female at whom he could look, but must not touch, the temptation was strong, too strong.

She kissed him full on the mouth.

Her breath was sweet and spicy, intoxicating.

She was woman and he was man, and all that stood in the way of consummation was his hampering clothing. Her hands were at the fastenings of his trousers but fumbling inexpertly. Reluctantly he removed his own from her full buttocks to assist her, was dimly conscious of the cold stone under his naked rump as the garment was pushed down to his knees, was ecstatically conscious of the enveloping warmth of her as she mounted him and rode him, not violently but languorously, slowly, slowly. . .

The tension releasing explosion came.

She slumped against him, over him, her nipples brushing his face. Gently, reluctantly she rolled off his body. He felt her hand at his mouth. It held a large piece of the fungus. He took it from her fingers, chewed and swallowed. It was even better than his first taste of it had been.

He drifted into sleep.

86

Chapter 19

He dreamed.

In the dream he was a child.

He was one of the *Lode Venturer* survivors who had made the long trek south from the vicinity of the north magnetic pole. He could remember the crash landing, the swift and catastrophic conversion of what had been a little, warm, secure world into twisted, crumpled wreckage.

He remembered the straggling column of men, women and children burdened with supplies from the wrecked gaussjammer—food, sacks of precious Terran seed grain, sealed stasis containers of the fertilized ova of Terran livestock, the incubators broken down into portable components, the parts of the solar power generator.

He was one of *Lode Venturer's* people who had survived both crash landing and long march, who had found the valley, who had tilled the fields and planted the grain, who had worked at setting up the incubating equipment. Although only a child he had shared the fears of his elders as the precious store of preserved provisions dwindled and the knowledge that, in spite of strict rationing, it would not last out until the harvest, until the incubators delivered progenitors of future herds of meat animals.

He remembered the day of the drawing of lots.

There were the losers—three young men, a middle-aged woman and another one who was little more than a girl—standing there, frightened yet somehow proud, while further lots were drawn to decide who would be executioner and butcher. A fierce argument had developed—some of the women claiming, belatedly, that females of child-bearing age should have been exempt from the first lottery. While this was going on another boy—the son of the middle-aged woman, came down from the caves to which he had run rather than watch his mother slaughtered. He was bearing an armful of the fungus.

"Food!" he was shouting. "Food! I have tasted it and it is good!"

They had all sung a hymn of thanksgiving then, grateful for their delivery from what, no matter how necessary to their survival, would have been a ghastly sin.

Bread of Heaven, bread of Heaven,
Feed me till I want no more, want no more,
Feed me till I want no more. . .

He awoke then, drifting slowly up from the warm, deep sleep. He did what he had to do, relieving the pressure on bowels and bladder as he lay there. He wondered dimly why people ever went to the trouble of fabricating elaborate sanitary arrangements. The fungus needed his body wastes. He needed the fungus. It was all so simple.

He reached out and grabbed another handful of the satisfying, intoxicating stuff. He became aware that the woman—or a woman—was with him. While he was still eating they coupled.

He slept.

He dreamed.

He was the Pastor, the leader of the people of the settlement.

He had looked over the arrangements for the feast and all was well. There was an ample supply of the strong liquor brewed and distiled from grain—the last harvest had been a good one, surplus to food requirements. Pigs had been slaughtered and dressed, ready for the roasting. Great baskets of the fungus had been brought down from the caves. Since it had been discovered that it thrived on human manure it had proliferated, spreading from the original cavern through the entire subterranean complex. Perhaps it had changed, too. It seemed that with every passing year its flavor had improved. At first—he seemed to remember—it had been almost tasteless although filling and nutritious.

But now. . .

The guests from the ship, clattering through the night sky in their noisy flying boats, were dropping down to the village. He hoped that there would not be the same trouble as there had been with the guests from that other ship, the one with the odd name, *Epsilon Pavonis*. Of course, it had not been the guests themselves who had made the trouble; it had been their captain. But *this* captain, he had been told, was himself a True Follower. All should be well.

All was well.

The love feast, the music, the dancing, the singing of the old, familiar hymns. . .

And the love. . .

And surely the manna, the gift from the all-wise, all-loving God of the True Followers, was better than it ever had been. What need was there, after all, for the corn liquor, the roast pig?

Bread of Heaven, bread of Heaven,
Feed me till I want no more. . .

He walked slowly through and among the revellers, watching benevolently the fleshly intermingling of his own people and those from the starship. It was. . . *good*. Everything was good. He exchanged a few words with the Survey Service petty officer who, dutifully operating his equipment, was making a visual and sound recording of the feast. He wondered briefly why the man was amused when he said that the pictures and the music would be acclaimed when presented in the tabernacles of the True Followers on Earth and other planets. He looked benignly at the group at which the camera was aimed—a plump, naked, supine crewman being fondled by three children. It was a charming scene.

And why the strong sensation of déjà vu?

Why the brief, gut-wrenching disgust?

He heard the distant hammering in the still, warm air, growing louder and louder. More airboats—what did they call them? pinnaces?—from the ship, he thought. Perhaps the captain himself, Commander Belton, was coming after all. He would be pleased to see for himself how well his fellow True Followers on this distant world had kept the faith. . .

Then the dream became a nightmare.

There was shouting and screaming.

There was fighting.

There were armed men discharging their weapons indiscriminately, firing on both their own shipmates and the colonists.

There was his confrontation with a tall, gaunt, stiffly uniformed man.

(Again the flash of déjà vu.)

There were the bitter, angry words.

"True Followers, you call yourselves? I understood that my people had been invited to a religious service. . . And I find a disgusting orgy in progress!"

"But we are True Followers! We were saved. God Himself sent his manna to save us from committing the deadliest sin of all. Here! Taste! Eat and believe!"

89

And a hand smashed viciously down, striking the proferred manna from his grasp, as Belton shouted, "Keep that filthy muck away from me!"

He saw the muzzle of a pistol pointing at him, saw the flare of energy that jolted him into oblivion.

He slowly drifted up to semi-consciousness. There was a woman. There was more of the manna.

Again he slept.

Chapter 20

He dreamed.

He dreamed that a bright, harsh light was beating through his closed eyelids, that something hard was nudging him in the ribs.

He opened his eyes, immediately shut them again before he was blinded.

A voice, a somehow familiar female voice, was saying, "Captain Grimes! Captain Grimes! Wake up, damn you!" And then, in an intense whisper, "Oh! If you could only see yourself!"

He muttered, "Go 'way. Go 'way."

"Captain Grimes! John!" There was a hand on his shoulder, shaking him. He opened his eyes again. She had put her flashlight on the ground so that now he saw her by its reflected light. She was a woman. She was beautiful—but so was everybody in this enchanted cavern. He dimly recognized her.

She said, "I must get you out of here."

Why? he wondered. *Why?*

She got her hands under his naked shoulders, tried to lift him. He got his hands about her shoulders, pulled her down. She struggled, kneeing him in the groin. He let go and she stood up, stepping back from him. The shirt had been torn from her upper body. In spite of the pain that she had inflicted on him he felt a surge of desire, reached out for her exposed breasts. She stepped back another pace.

He wanted her—but to get up to go after her was too much trouble.

But he muttered, "Do'n' go . . . Do'n' go . . . I . . . want . . . you . . . always . . . wanted . . . you . . ."

Her face was glistening oddly. Dimly he realized that she was weeping. She said, "Not *here*. Not *now*. Pull yourself together. Come back to the ship."

He said—the words were coming more easily now, but were they his? "I . . . hate . . . ships . . . All . . . True

91

. . . Followers . . . hate . . . ships . . . Stay . . . here . . . Be . . . happy . . ."

Her face and voice hardened. She said, "I'll get you out of here by force!"

He was fast losing interest in the conversation. He reached out languidly from the omnipresent manna, chewed and swallowed.

He muttered, "Try . . . this . . . Make . . . you . . . human . . ."

But she was gone.

It did not matter.

The warmth of the communal life of the cavern surrounded him.

There were women.

And always there was the manna.

He slept.

He dreamed.

He was one of the crowd being harangued by the Pastor.

"We must sever all ties with Earth!" he heard. "We are the true, the real True Followers! Were we not saved by God himself from death and from deadly sin? But these Earthmen, who have intruded into our paradise, who have strayed from the true path, refuse to believe . . ."

"So burn the houses, my people! Destroy everything that links us to faithless Earth, even our herds and our crops!

"God's own manna is all that we need, all that we shall ever need!"

And somebody else—Grimes knew that it was one of the community's physicians—was crying over and over, in a sort of ecstasy, "Holy symbiosis! Holy symbiosis!"

Crackling flames and screaming pigs and the voices of the people, singing,

Bread of Heaven, bread of Heaven,
Feed me till I want no more, want no more . . .

Again the too bright light and again the hand shaking his shoulder . . .

"Wake up, John! Wake up!"

"Go 'way . . ."

"John! Look at me!"

He opened his eyes.

She had placed her torch on a ledge so that it shone full upon her. She was naked. Diamonds gleamed in the braided coronet of the hair of her head and even in the heart-shaped growth at the scission of her thighs. She was a spaceman's pin-up girl in the warm, living flesh.

She said softly, "You want me. You shall have me—but not here, among these degenerates, this filth." She turned slowly, saying, "Follow . . ."

Almost he made the effort to get to his feet but it was too much trouble. With faint stirrings of regret he watched her luminous body swaying away from him. Once she turned and beckoned. He wondered vaguely why she should be wearing such an angry expression. And before she reached the mouth of the cave he had fallen back into sleep.

A long while or a little while—he had no way of knowing—later he awoke. After a few mouthfuls of manna he crawled until he found a woman.

And slept again.

And dreamed.

Subtly the dreams changed.

There were, as before, memories from the minds of the colonists who had long lived in symbiosis with the fungus but there were now other memories—brief flashes, indistinct at first but all the time increasing in clarity and duration. There were glimpses of the faces and the bodies of women whom he had known—Jane Pentecost, Maggie Lazenby, Ellen Russell, Una Freeman, Maya . . .

The women . . .

And the ships.

Lines from a long-ago read and long-ago forgotten piece of verse drifted through his mind:

The arching sky is calling
Spacemen back to their trade . . .

He was sitting in the control room of his first command, the little Serpent Class courier *Adder*, a king at last even though his realm, to others, was a very insignificant one. Obedient to the touch of his fingers on the console the tiny ship lifted from the Lindisfarne Base apron.

All hands! Stand by! Free Falling!
The lights below us fade . . .

And through the dream, louder and louder, surged the arhythmic hammering of a spaceship's inertial drive.

He awoke.

He scooped a handful of manna from a nearby clump.

He chewed, swallowed.

Somehow it was not the same as it had been; there was a

93

hint of bitterness, a rancidity. He relieved himself where he lay and then crawled over and among the recumbent bodies until he found a receptive woman.

Like a great, fat slug . . . he thought briefly.

(But what was a slug? Surely nothing like this beautiful creature . . .)

After he was finished with her and she with him he drifted again into sleep, even though that mechanical clangor coming from somewhere outside the cave was a growing irritation.

He dreamed more vividly than before.

He had just brought *Discovery* down to a landing in the Paddington Oval on Botany Bay. His officers and the Marine guard behind him, he was marching down the ramp to the vividly green grass. Against the pale blue sky he could see the tall, white flagstaffs, each with its rippling ensign, dark blue with the cruciform constellation of silver stars in the fly, with the superimposed red, white and blue crosses in the upper canton.

There was a band playing.

He was singing in time to the familiar tune:
Waltzing Matilda, Waltzing Matilda,
You'll come a-waltzing Matilda with me . . .
He awoke.

There was still that arythmic hammering, drifting in from somewhere outside—but the music, vastly amplified almost drowned the mechanical racket.

Up jumped the swagman, sprang into the billabong,
"You'll never catch me alive!" cried he . . .

And what was this noisome billabong into which he, Grimes, had plunged? Would his ghost still be heard after he was gone from it? Would his memories of Deep Space and the ships plying the star lanes remain to haunt the swinish dreamers of Farhaven? Would that honest old national song replace the phoney piety of the True Followers' hymn?

Manna! he thought disgustedly, kicking out at a dim-glowing mass. It splattered under his bare foot and the stench was sickening. He was seized with an uncontrollable spasm of nausea. Drained and shaken he stumbled toward the cave entrance, the music luring him on as though he were one of the Pied Piper's rats. He tripped over sleeping bodies. A woman clutched his ankle. He looked down at her. He could not be sure but he thought that she was the one responsible for his original downfall. Almost he brought his free foot smashing down on to her sleepily smiling face but, at the last moment, desisted.

She was what she was, just as he was what he was—and he had wallowed in the mire happily enough . . .

He stooped and with both hands gently disengaged her fingers.

He staggered on, finally out onto the ledge. The sunlight blinded him. Then at last he was able to see her, hanging above the valley, beautiful and brightly golden, *The Far Traveler*. It was from her that the music was blaring. It ceased suddenly, was replaced by the amplified voice of Big Sister.

"I am sending the pinnace for you, Captain Grimes. It will come as closely alongside the cliff as possible. The robots will help you aboard."

He waited there, naked and filthy and ashamed, until the boat came for him.

Chapter 21

Grimes—clean, clothed, depilated but still shaky—sat in the Baroness's salon telling his story. She listened in silence, as did the omnipresent Big Sister.

When he was finished Big Sister said, "I must make a further analysis of the fungus specimens. Drug addiction among human and other intelligent life forms is not unusual, of course, but the symbiotic aspects of this case intrigue me."

"And the dreams," said Grimes. "The dreams . . . I must have experienced the entire history of the Lost Colony . . ."

"For years," said Big Sister, "the fungus has been nourished by the waste products of the colonists' bodies—and when they have died it has been nourished by the bodies themselves. It has become, in some way that I have yet to discover, the colonists. Is there not an old saying: A man is what he eats? This could be true for other living beings. And the symbiosis has been more, much more, than merely physical. By eating the fungus you, for a while, entered into the symbiotic relationship."

"Very interesting," commented Grimes. "But you must have known what was happening to me, even if not why or how. You should have sent in the robots to drag me out by force."

"Command decisions are not my prerogative," said Big Sister smugly. "Her Excellency did suggest that I attempt a forcible rescue but I dissuaded her. It was a matter for humans only, for humans to resolve for themselves, essentially for a human of your sort to resolve for himself. I know very well, Captain Grimes, how you hate robots, how your dislike for me has prevented you from being properly grateful for your rescue from Commander Delamere's clutches." There was a brief, almost human chuckle. "I did think that Her Excellency would be able to recapture you by the use of a *very* human bait, but her attempt was not successful . . ."

Grimes looked at the Baroness, remembering her as he had seen her. His ears burned as he flushed miserably. If she were

96

embarrassed by her own memory of the occasion she did not show it.

"So," went on Big Sister, "I made use of what I have learned of your peculiar psychology—your professional pride, your rather childish nationalism, your very real love of ships." She paused, then said, "A man who loves ships can't be all bad."

"A man," said the Baroness coldly, "who could refuse what I offered can't be all man."

He said, "I am sorry. I am truly sorry. But I was under the influence of the . . . manna . . ."

She said, "In vino veritas, Captain Grimes. And worst of all is the knowledge that the cacophony of a ship's engines, the trite music of a folksong about an Australian sheep stealer, succeeded where I failed. I will tell you now that I had intended that a relationship—not permanent but mutually satisfying—would develop between us. There is little likelihood now that this will come to pass. Our relations will remain as they have been since I first engaged you, those between employer and employee."

She turned away from Grimes, addressed the playmaster. "Take us up, Big Sister, up and away from this planet. I prefer not to remain on a world where I was unable successfully to compete with drug sodden degenerates or with an unhuman electronic intelligence."

Grimes wondered if Big Sister was feeling as resentful as he was himself. Probably not, he thought. Nonhuman electronic intelligences must surely be unemotional.

Chapter 22

So *The Far Traveler* lifted from Farhaven, with Grimes far less in actual command of the vessel than he ever had been, proceeding in the general direction of the Shakespearian Sector, out toward the rim of the galaxy.

It was quite a while before the after effects of the drug wore off and until they did so Grimes was treated as a convalescent. It was during this period that he noticed a subtle change in Big Sister's attitude toward him. He had, almost from the start, envisaged her as a bossy, hard-featured woman, hating and despising men. Now the imaginary flesh with which he clothed the electronic intelligence was that of an aunt whom, during his childhood, he had liked rather than loved, feared slightly, obeyed (for most of the time) during a period when his parents, away traveling, had left him in her charge. He recalled the unsuspected soft side of her nature which she had exhibited when he had been confined to his bed for some days after he had made a crash landing in the hot-air balloon that he had constructed himself, suffering two broken ribs and a fractured ankle.

She had pampered him then, just as Big Sister was pampering him now (and as the Baroness most certainly was not). Nonetheless, a year or so later, he had been very surprised when this aunt had embarked upon a whirlwind romance with a Dog Star Line second mate who was enjoying a spell of shore leave on Earth, returning with this spaceman to his home world. (Now, he thought, remembering, he would not have been surprised. As a child he had regarded the lady as a dragon but she had been the sort of tall, lean auburn-haired woman that the adult Grimes always fell for.)

Much as Big Sister reminded him of this aunt, thought Grimes, he could not imagine her eloping with anybody or anything. He supposed that, having saved him, she regarded herself as being responsible for him.

Eventually, when Big Sister decided that he was functioning as well as he ever would function, he was bidden to the Baroness's presence.

The lady said, "I am informed that I once again can enjoy the services of my yachtmaster. Can you, out of your long and wide experience in the Survey Service, suggest our next port of call?"

He thought hard then said doubtfully, "Kinsolving?"

"Kinsolving," she stated, "is not a Lost Colony." (She must have been having a good rummage in Big Sister's memory bank.) "It is one of the Rim Worlds. For some reason the colony was abandoned. There are now no people there at all. The object of my research, as well you know, is social evolution in the Lost Colonies. How can there be social evolution when there is nobody to evolve?"

Grimes tried not to sigh too audibly. He was never at home in this lushly appointed Owner's Suite or in the comic opera uniform that he was obliged to wear during these audiences. He would have been far happier in his own quarters. At least there he could smoke his pipe in peace. But his employer did not approve of smoking. Fortunately she did not disapprove of the use of drugs other than tobacco, such as alcohol—and, Grimes was bound to admit, her robot butler mixed a superb dry martini. He was appreciating the one that he was sipping; Big Sister had at last given him permission to drink again.

He looked at her over the frosted rim of his glass. She was reclining gracefully on her chaise longue, looking (as always) like a rather superior version of Goya's *Maja*. She looked at him very coldly. He realized that the top tunic button of his gold and purple livery was undone. He did it up.

She said, "You aren't much use, Captain, are you? I thought, in my girlish innocence, that an ex-Commander of the Interstellar Federation's Survey Service would have been the ideal captain for an expedition such as this. I know that you, before you resigned your commission, discovered at least three Lost Colonies. There were New Sparta and Morrowvia, both of which we shall, eventually, be visiting. And there was, of course, Botany Bay. With reference to the first two worlds it will be interesting to see what effects your clumsy meddlings have had upon the lives of the unspoiled peoples of those planets . . ."

Grimes was acutely conscious of the burning flush that suffused his prominent ears. He, personally, would hardly have classed either the New Spartans or the Morrowvians as unspoiled—and New Sparta had been on the brink of a devas-

99

tating civil war at the time of his landing. As for Morrowvia—he had not been the only interfering outsider. There had been the Dog Star Line's Captain Danzellan, looking after the commercial interests of his principals. There had been the piratical Drongo Kane in his own *Southerly Buster*, looking after his own interests.

"And didn't you enjoy a liaison with one of the local rulers on Morrowvia?" continued the Baroness. "I find it hard to understand—but then, I have never been enamored of cats."

Maya, remembered Grimes. *Feline ancestry but very much a woman—not like this cold, rich bitch* . . . Then he hated himself for the uncharitable thought. He owed the Baroness much. Had it not been for her intervention he would have been haled back to Lindisfarne to stand trial. And to have done what she had done in that vile cave on Farhaven must have required considerable resolution. He could hardly blame her for blaming him for the failure of that second rescue attempt.

Nonetheless he said, with some indignation, "I was under the impression, Your Excellency, that my full and frank report on the happenings on Morrowvia was not to be released to the general public."

"*I* am not the general public," she said. "Money, Captain Grimes, is the key that will open the door to any vault in the Galaxy. Your friend, Commander Delamere, was, I think, more impressed by my wealth than my beauty. There are many others like him."

Grimes missed the chance of saying something gallant.

"Your Excellency, may I interrupt?" asked Big Sister, her voice coming from everywhere and nowhere.

"You have already interrupted," said the Baroness. "But continue."

"Your Excellency, I have monitored Carlotti transmissions from the Admiralty, on Earth, to all Survey Service ships and bases . . ."

Have you? thought Grimes. *Restricted wavebands, unbreakable codes . . . And what are they against, the power of money?*

"A distress message capsule was picked up off Lentimure by the Survey Service destroyer *Acrux*. It originated from a ship called *Lode Ranger*. Text is as follows: Pile dead. Proceeding under diesel power. Intend landing on apparently habitable planet . . ."

There was more—a listing of crew and passengers, what astronomical data might just possibly be of use to future rescuers. In very few cases, Grimes knew, was such information of any value—but a modern computer, given the elements of a capsule's trajectory, could determine with some accuracy its departure point. And then the rescue ship, arriving a few centuries after the call for assistance, would find either a thriving Lost Colony or, after a search, the eroded wreckage of the lost ship and, possibly, a few human skeletons.

Grimes asked, "Do you have the coordinates of the departure point?"

Big Sister replied, "Apparently they are yet to be determined, Captain. As soon as they are transmitted by the Admiralty I shall inform you."

The Baroness said, "It just could happen that we shall be the nearest ship to the Lost Colony. It would be interesting to make the first landing upon such a world, before the clumsy boots of oafish spacemen have trampled all sorts of valuable evidence into the dust."

Grimes said, "Probably the Lost Colony, if there is one, is halfway across the Galaxy from here."

She said, "You are unduly pessimistic, Captain. Never forget that chance plays a great part in human life. And now, while we are waiting, could you refresh my memory regarding the gaussjammers and how it was that so many of them originated Lost Colonies?"

You probably know more about it than I do, thought Grimes. *After all, it's you that's writing the thesis.*

He said, "The gaussjammers, using the Ehrenhaft Drive, were the ships of the Second Expansion. Prior to them were the so-called Deep Freeze ships which, of course, were not faster than light. The gaussjammers, though, were FTL. With the Ehrenhaft generators in operation they were, essentially, huge monopoles. They tried to be in two places at once along a line of magnetic force, proceeding along such tramlines to their destinations. They were extremely vulnerable to magnetic storms; a really severe one could fling them thousands of light-years off course. There was another effect, too. The micro-piles upon which they relied for power would be drained of all energy. The captain of a gaussjammer lost in space, his pile dead, had only one course of action open to him. He used his emergency diesels to power the Ehrenhaft generators. He proceeded in what he hoped would be the right direction. When he ran out of diesel fuel his biochemist would convert what should have been food for the ship's company into more fuel.

"Finally, if he was lucky, he found a planet before food

101

and fuel ran out. If his luck still held he managed to land in one piece. And then, if conditions were not too impossible, he and his people stood a fair chance of founding a Lost Colony . . ."

Big Sister spoke again. "I have intercepted and decoded more signals. I estimate that we can be in orbit about *Lode Ranger's* planet no more than ten standard days from now. As far as I can ascertain there are no Survey Service vessels in our vicinity; it is a reasonable assumption that we shall make the first landing. Have I your permission to adjust trajectory?"

"Of course," said the Baroness. "Adjust trajectory as soon as the captain and myself are in our couches."

"I should be in the control room," said Grimes.

"Is that really necessary?" asked the Baroness.

Big Sister adjusted trajectory, shutting down inertial drive and Mannschenn Drive, using the directional gyroscopes to swing the ship about her axes, lining her up on the target star. Grimes, sweating it out in his bunk, did not doubt that due and proper allowance was being made for galactic drift. He was obliged to admit that Big Sister could do everything that he could do, and at least as well—but *he* should have been doing it. (That aunt of his who had run away with the Sirian spaceman had annoyed the young Grimes more than once by doing the things that he thought that he should have been doing.) He listened to the cold yet not altogether mechanical voice making the routine announcements: "Stopping inertial drive. Stand by for free fall . . . Mannschenn Drive—*off.*" There was the usual sensation of spatial and temporal disorientation. "Directional gyroscopes—*on.* Prepare for centrifugal effects . . . Directional gyroscopes— *off.* Mannschenn Drive—restarting." And the low hum, rising to a thin, high whine as the spinning rotors built up speed, precessing, tumbling down the dark dimensions . . . And the colors, sagging down the spectrum, and the distorted, warped perspective . . . And, as often happened, the transitory flash of déjà vu . . . This was happening now, had happened before, would happen again but . . . differently. In some other Universe, on a previous coil of time—or, perhaps, on a coil of time yet to be experienced—he had married the Princess Marlene, the father of whose sons he was, on El Dorado, had been accepted by the aristocratic and opulent inhabitants of that planet as one of the family, a member of the club and, eventually, using his wife's money, had caused the space-yacht, *The Far Traveler,* to be built to his own specifications. He was both Owner and Master. He was—but briefly, briefly, in that alternate universe—a truly contented man.

And then outlines ceased to waver, colors to fade, intensify and shift, and he was . . . himself.

He was John Grimes, disgraced ex-Commander, late of the Federation's Survey Service, Master *de jure* but not *de facto* of a ship that was no more—or was she more, much more, but not in any way that conceivably could benefit him?—than the glittering toy of an overly rich, discontented woman.

"On trajectory," said Big Sister, "for *Lode Ranger's* planet. Normal routine may be resumed."

"I am coming up to Control," said Grimes.

"You may come up to Control," said Big Sister, making it sound as though she was granting a great favor.

Chapter 23

The Far Traveler fell through the warped continuum toward the yellow sun on one of whose planets *Lode Ranger's* people had found refuge. She was alone and lonely, with no traffic whatsoever within range of her mass proximity indicator. Distant Carlotti signals were monitored by Big Sister and, according to her, no ship was closer than the destroyer *Acrux*—and she was one helluva long way away.

Nonetheless Grimes was not happy. He said, "I know, Your Excellency, that with the advent of Carlotti Radio it is no longer mandatory to carry a Psionic Communications Officer—but I think that you should have shipped one."

"Have a prying telepath aboard my ship, Captain Grimes?" she flared. "Out of the question! It is bad enough being compelled by archaic legislation to employ a human yachtmaster."

Grimes sighed. He said, "As you know, PCOs are carried aboard all Survey Service vessels and in the ships of most other navies. They are required to observe the code of ethics formulated by the Rhine Institute. But today their function is not that of ship to ship or ship to planet communication. They are, primarily, a sort of psychic radar. How shall I put it? This way, perhaps. You're making a landing on a strange world. Are the natives likely to be friendly or hostile? Unless the indigenes' way of thinking is too alien your PCO will be able to come up with the answer. If *The Far Traveler* carried a PCO we should already have some sort of idea of what we shall find on *Lode Ranger's* planet. Come to that, a PCO would have put us wise to the state of affairs on Farhaven and saved us from a degrading experience."

"I would prefer that you did not remind me of it," she said. "Meanwhile we shall just have to rely upon the highly efficient electronic equipment with which this ship is furnished."

She finished her drink. Grimes finished his. Obviously there was not going to be another.

She said, "Don't let me keep you from your dinner, Captain."

Grimes left her boudoir and went up to his own spartan—but only relatively so—quarters.

Not very long afterward *The Far Traveler* hung in orbit about *Lode Ranger's* world. It was inhabited without doubt; the lights of cities could be seen through the murky atmosphere of the night hemisphere and on the daylit face were features too regular to be natural, almost certainly roads and railways and canals. And those people had radio; the spaceship's NST receivers picked up an unceasing stream of signals. There was music. There were talks.

But . . .

But the music bore no resemblance to anything composed by Terrans for Terran ears and the instruments were exclusively percussion. There were complex rhythms, frail, tinkling melodies, not displeasing but alien, alien . . .

And the voices . . .

Guttural croaks, strident squeals, speaking no language known to Grimes or the Baroness, no tongue included in Big Sister's fantastically comprehensive data bank.

But that wasn't all.

The active element of the planet's atmosphere was chlorine.

"There will be no Lost Colony here, Your Excellency," said Grimes. "*Lode Ranger's* captain would never have landed once his spectroscopic analysis told him what to expect. He must have carried on."

"Even so," she said, "I have found a new world. I have ensured for myself a place in history." She smiled in self mockery. "For what it is worth. Now that we are here our task will be to carry out a preliminary survey."

"Do you intend to land, Your Excellency?" asked Big Sister.

"Of course."

"Then I must advise against it. You assumed, as did my builders, that my golden hull would be immune to corrosion. But somehow nobody took into account the possibility of a landing on a planet with a chlorine atmosphere. I have already detected traces of nitrohydrochloric acid which, I need hardly remind you, is a solvent for both gold and platinum."

"Only traces," said Grimes.

"Only traces, Captain," agreed Big Sister. "But would *you*

105

care to run naked through a forest in which there might be pockets of dichlorethyl sulfide?"

Grimes looked blank.

"Mustard gas," said Big Sister.

"Oh," said Grimes.

The Baroness said, "I am rich, as you know. Nonetheless this ship is a considerable investment. I do not wish her shell plating to be corroded, thus detracting from her value."

"Yes, it would spoil her good looks," admitted Grimes. But the main function of a ship, any ship, is not to look pretty. He remembered that long-ago English admiral who had frowned upon gunnery practice because it discolored the gleaming paintwork of the warcraft under his command.

He asked, "Couldn't you devise some sort of protective coating? A spray-on plastic. . ."

Big Sister replied, "I have already done so. And, anticipating that you and Her Excellency would wish to make a landing, the smaller pinnace has been treated, also your spacesuits and six of the general purpose robots. Meanwhile I have processed the photographs taken during our circumpolar orbits and, if you will watch the playmaster, I shall exhibit one that seems of especial interest."

Grimes and the Baroness looked at the glowing screen. There—dull, battered, corroded but still, after all these many years, recognizable—was the pear-shaped hull of a typical gaussjammer. Not far from it was a dome, obviously not a natural feature of the terrain, possibly evidence that the survivors had endeavored to set up some sort of settlement in the hostile environment. A few kilometers to the north was a fair-sized town.

"Could they—or their descendants—still be living, Captain?" asked the Baroness.

"People have lived in similar domes, on Earth's airless moon, for many generations," said Grimes. "And the Selenites could always pack up and return to Earth if they didn't like it. *Lode Ranger's* personnel had no place else to go."

"But . . . To live among aliens?"

"There are all sorts of odd enclaves throughout the Galaxy," said Grimes.

"Very well, Captain. We shall go down at once, to find what we shall find."

"Big Sister," asked Grimes, "assuming that we leave the ship now, what time of day will it be at the wreck when we land?"

"Late afternoon," was the reply.

"We should make a dawn landing," said Grimes.

"You are not in the Survey Service now, Captain," the Baroness told him. "You may as well forget Survey Service S.O.P."

"Those survivors—if there are any survivors—have waited for generations," said Grimes. "A few more hours won't hurt them."

"*I* am going down *now*," she told him. "You may come if you wish."

Grimes wished that he knew more about Space Law as applicable to civilian vessels. When is a captain not a captain? When he has his owner on board, presumably.

He said, "Shall we get into our spacesuits, Your Excellency? We shall need them if we leave the pinnace."

She said, "I will meet you in the boat bay, Captain."

Chapter 24

His robot stewardess helped him on with his spacesuit. The protective garment was no longer gold but, after the anti-corrosive spray, a dull, workmanlike grey. He preferred it in that color. He buckled on the belt with the two holstered pistols—one laser, one projectile. He checked the weapons to make sure they were models with firing studs instead of triggers, designed to be held in a heavily gauntletted hand. All was in order.

He went down to the boat bay. The Baroness was already there, clad as he was. Six of the general purpose robots were there. Golden, their asexual bodies had been beautiful; gray, they looked menacing, sinister. So did the pinnace.

"Should we get into trouble," said Grimes, speaking into his helmet microphone, "please come down for us." He could not resist adding, "if you get tarnished it will be just too bad."

"There was no need for that," said the Baroness. Through the helmet phones her voice was even more coldly metallic than that of the computer-pilot.

"Understood," said Big Sister shortly.

"Robots into the boat," ordered Grimes.

The automata filed into and through the airlock.

"After you, Your Excellency."

The Baroness, looking not unlike a robot herself, boarded.

Grimes followed her, took his seat in the pilot's chair. The airlock doors closed before he could bring a finger to the appropriate button. If Big Sister insisted on doing the things that he was being paid to do, that was all right by him.

He said, "One kilometer from the wreck please revert to manual control. My control."

"Understood, Captain," said Big Sister.

"Must you dot every 'i' and cross every 't'?" asked the Baroness crossly.

The boat's inertial drive grumbled itself awake; the boat bay doors opened. Through the aperture glowed the sunlit hemisphere of *Lode Ranger's* planet, a gigantic, clouded emerald. Then they were out and away from the ship, driving down rather than merely falling. Grimes kept his paws off the controls, although it required a considerable effort of will to refrain from touching them. Big Sister knew what she was doing, he told himself. He hoped.

Down they drove, down, down. The whispering of atmosphere along the hull became audible above the clatter of the inertial drive. There was no rise of cabin temperature although, thought Grimes, the cooling system must be working overtime. And, he told himself, the modified metal of which the pinnace was constructed had a far higher melting point than that of normal gold.

Down they drove, through high, green, wispy clouds.

Down they drove, and the land was spread out below them—mountain masses, seas, rivers, the long, straight line of a transcontinental railway, cities, forests . . .

Ahead of them and below something was flying. A bird? Grimes studied it through his binoculars, wondering how he had come to make such a gross underestimation of its size. It was a huge, delta-winged aircraft. It pursued its course steadily, ignoring the intruder from space. Probably its pilot did not know that there were strangers in his sky.

The radar altimeter was unwinding more slowly now. They were low enough to make out features of the landscape with the naked eye. Ahead of them was the town, the small city, its architecture obviously alien. The proportions of the buildings were all wrong by human standards and not one of the many towers was perpendicular; the truncated spires leaned toward and away from each other at drunken angles.

They swept over the town. Beyond it was the wreck of the ancient Terran spaceship and beyond that the discolored white dome. Through his binoculars Grimes could see spacesuited figures standing by the airlock of the vessel. *Men* in spacesuits? They had to be human; the natives would not require protective clothing on their own planet.

But what were they doing?

Fighting?

Yes, they were fighting—the spacemen and the near-naked, humanoid but far from human natives. It was hand to hand almost, at close range with pistols from the muzzles of which came flashes of bright flame. Oddly enough there seemed to be no casualties on either side.

Yet.

"We have come in the nick of time," said the Baroness. "If we had waited until local daybreak, as *you* suggested . . ."

There was a screwy lack of logic about what she was saying, about the entire situation. If *Lode Ranger* had just landed the situation would have made sense, but . . . The gaussjammer had not come down today, or yesterday, or the day before that.

"I relinquish control, Captain," came the voice of Big Sister. "You are now one kilometer from the wreck."

Grimes brought his gloved hands up to the console.

"*Do* something," ordered the Baroness. "There are people, humans, there, being murdered."

The pinnace was not armed. (If Grimes, man of peace as he claimed to be, had had any say in the building of *The Far Traveler* and her ancillary craft she would have been.) Even had she been fitted with weaponry Grimes would have been unable to fire into that melee with any degree of discrimination. All that he could do was to bring her in fast, fast and noisily. The combatants heard the rapidly approaching clangor; they would have had to have been stone deaf not to do so. They stopped fighting, looked up and around. Then they ran, all of them, human and autochthon. Together they fled, arms and legs pumping ludicrously, jostling each other at the open airlock door of the gaussjammer, scrambling for the safety of the interior of the old ship.

They were gone from sight, all of them, their dropped weapons, gleaming greenly in the light of the afternoon sun, littering the bare, sandy ground.

Grimes slammed the pinnace down hard at the foot of the ramp that protruded from the airlock door. With one hand he sealed his helmet, with the other he unsnapped his seat belt. Big Sister had already opened the inner airlock door. Two steps took him to the little chamber. The Baroness was with him. The inner door closed, the outer door opened. He jumped to the gound, pulling his pistols as he did so. She landed just behind him and then ran ahead.

"Hold it!" he called. "I'll send the robots in first to draw the fire. They're expendable."

"And you're not?" she asked coldly.

"Not if I can help it. And I'm not invulnerable either. Your tin soldiers are."

She admitted grudgingly that there was sense in what he said. They stood together, looking up at the huge, weathered hulk, the great, metallic peg top supported in an upright position by its landing struts. And what was happening inside the

110

battered hull? he wondered. Were the survivors of the wreck—the descendants of the survivors, rather—and the natives still fighting hand to hand along the alleyways, through the public rooms? His helmet muffled external sounds but did not deafen him completely. He listened but could hear no cries, no gunfire.

The first two robots emerged from the pinnace's airlock. He told them to board the ship, not to fire unless fired upon, to use stunguns rather than laser pistols, their net-throwing blunderbusses in preference to either.

When the automata were aboard he followed, climbing the rickety, warped ramp with caution. It had been damaged, he noticed, and clumsily patched with some dissimilar metal. The repairing plates had been riveted, not welded.

"Are you brave enough to go in?" asked the Baroness when they reached the head of the gangway.

Grimes did not answer her. He joined the two robots who were standing in the airlock chamber. They were using their laser pistols, set to low intensity, as torches, shining the beams in through the open inner door.

Grimes used his chin to nudge the controls of his suit's external speaker to maximum amplification. "Ahoy!" he shouted. *"Lode Ranger!* Ahoy! This is the Survey Service! We're here to rescue you!"

"We are *not* the Survey Service," snapped the Baroness.

Grimes ignored her. "Ahoy!" he called again. *"Lode Ranger,* ahoy!"

He could imagine the sound of his amplified voice rolling up and along the spiral alleyway, the ramp that in these ships encircled the hull from tapered stern to blunt, dome-shaped bows inboard of the inner skin.

There was no reply.

He said, "All right, we're going in. We'll follow the ramp all the way to the control room. Two robots ahead, then ourselves, then two robots to cover our rear. The remaining two will guard the airlock."

They began to climb.

It was a far from silent progress. At one time the deck had been coated with a rubbery plastic but, over the long years, it had perished, its decomposition no doubt hastened by the chlorine-rich atmosphere. The feet of the marching robots set up a rhythmic clangor, the heavy boots of the man and the woman made their own contributions to the rolling reverberation. It would have been impossible not to have stepped in time to the metallic drumbeat.

111

Up and around they marched, up and around. The low intensity laser beams probed dark openings—cross alleyways, the entrances to cabins and machinery spaces and public rooms. There were streakings in the all-pervasive dust suggestive of footprints, of scufflings, but nothing was definite. On one bulkhead was a great stain, old and evil. It could have been no more than a careless spillage of paint in the distant past but Grimes sensed that somebody—or something—had died there, messily.

He called a halt.

"Now we can hear ourselves think," commented the Baroness.

"Now we can hear," he agreed.

And there were sounds, faint and furtive, that would have been faint even without the muffling effect of their helmets. They seemed to come from ahead, they seemed to come from inside the ancient hull. And within the archaic ship, Grimes knew, there would be a veritable maze of alleyways and companionways, shafts vertical and horizontal. The only hope of capturing either a native or a descendant of the *Lode Ranger* survivors would be if any of them tried to escape through the airlock door, where the two robots he had detailed for that duty were on guard.

One of those robots spoke now—or it may have been Big Sister who spoke.

"Ground cars are approaching from the city. I suggest that you retreat to the pinnace."

Grimes hated to leave a job half finished, less than half finished, hardly begun in fact. But to remain in the ship could well prove suicidal. Still he waited so he could call, one last time, "*Lode Ranger*, ahoy! We have come to rescue you! Follow us to our boat!"

And then, wasting no time, the boarding party ran rather than walked down to the airlock.

Chapter 25

Somebody had gotten there before them. Somebody had tried to break past the robot sentries and was now entangled in the metallic mesh cast by a net-throwing blunderbuss, was still struggling ineffectually. It was a man in an archaic spacesuit, an ugly looking pistol in his right hand. Fortunately he could not bring this weapon to bear.

"Easy, friend, easy," said Grimes. "It's all right. Tell us about it in the pinnace."

But the man could not hear him, of course. His helmet looked as though it would deaden exterior sounds even more effectively than the one that Grimes was wearing. If his suit were equipped with radio, and if that radio were still functioning, it would not be likely that the frequency to which it was tuned would be the one being used by the party from *The Far Traveler.*

"Don't hurt him," ordered Grimes. "Take him to the boat."

He looked toward the city, to the column of dust midway between town and ship, the fast-traveling cloud that did not quite conceal betraying glints of metal. The ground cars, obviously, that Big Sister had reported. And they were wasting no time, whoever and whatever they were. The sooner he was in the pinnace and up and away the better. He would return, better armed and better prepared—but that was in the future. This was *now.* This was strategic retreat from heavier forces, from an enemy who had already opened fire from his armored vehicles with large caliber projectile weapons. A shell burst just short of the pinnace, another to one side of it.

"Run!" ordered Grimes.

The two robots with the prisoner between them broke into a gallop. Grimes and the Baroness followed, but less speedily. Spacesuits are not meant for running in. The other four robots brought up the rear.

The outer airlock door of the pinnace was already open.

113

The leading robots and the struggling man passed through just before a shell landed on the boat itself.

"Hell!" exclaimed Grimes.

"Don't . . . worry . . ." panted the Baroness. "She . . . can . . . take . . . it . . ."

The green smoke cleared and Grimes saw that the pinnace seemed to be undamaged, although bright gold gleamed where the protective plastic had been ripped away.

The next two rounds were wide and Grimes and the Baroness scrambled into the airlock during the brief lull. Another shell hit, however, as the last pair of robots were boarding. It was like, Grimes said later, being a bug inside a bass drum. But at the time he was not thinking up picturesque similes. He was getting upstairs, fast, before a chance projectile scored a hit on some vulnerable part of the pinnace. A similar craft in the Survey Service would have been fitted with armor shields for the viewpoints. This one was not. No doubt Big Sister would make good this omission but Grimes was more concerned with *now* than a possible future.

From his seat, as the boat lifted, he saw a squad of the reptilian humanoids jumping out of the leading, multi-wheeled land car. They carried weapons, firearms of some kind, took aim and delivered a ragged volley. It sounded like hail on a tin roof. The bullets were no more effective than the shells had been.

They went on firing after the pinnace was airborne and even when she was well aloft there was a sharp *ping* on her underside.

"Did you look at them?" demanded the Baroness. "Giants. At least twice as big as the ones we first saw!"

"We were lucky to get away," said Grimes. "So was our friend here—although he didn't seem to want to be rescued."

"The robots frightened him," she said. "To him they're monsters. . ."

"Big Sister," said Grimes. "Over to you. Get us back on board as soon as possible."

"I have control, Captain," came the reply from the transceiver.

Grimes released himself from his seat, went to the cabin at the rear of the pinnace. The Baroness accompanied him.

She whispered, "He's . . . dead . . ."

"Only fainted," said Grimes. Then, to the robots, "Get the net off him."

They looked down at the spacesuited man sprawled on the

deck. Grimes sneezed suddenly; there was an irritating acridity in the air despite the efforts of the ventilating fans. He knelt by the still figure. He was amazed to find that the suit was made only from thin, coarsely woven cloth. But, he reasoned, for many years *Lode Ranger's* people and their descendants must have had to make do with whatever materials came to hand. He looked at the ovate, opaque helmet, tried to see through the narrow, glazed vision slit to the face beneath.

But the slit was not glazed.

It was not glazed and there were other openings, approximately where ears and mouth are located on a human head. A dreadful suspicion was growing in his mind.

He took hold of the helmet with his two hands, gave it a half turn to the left. It resisted the twisting motion. He tried to turn it to the right. It still would not come free. So he just lifted it.

He stared down in horror at the big-domed, saurian head, at the dull, sightless, faceted eyes, at the thin-lipped mouth, twisted in a silent snarl, from which ropy slime still dribbled.

He heard the Baroness's gasp of horrified dismay.

He let the dead, ugly head drop to the deck, picked up the glittering, vicious looking pistol. The trigger guard was big enough for him to get his gloved forefinger into it.

"Don't!" the Baroness cried sharply.

He ignored her, pulled the trigger. A stream of bright but harmless sparks flashed from the muzzle of the gun.

"A toy . . ." she whispered. "But what . . .?"

He asked, "Did you ever, as a child, play cowboys and Indians, Your Excellency? No, I don't suppose you did. But you must have heard of the game. And that's what these . . . kids were playing. But they'd call the game invaders and people or something like that, with the invaders as the baddies. Just a re-enactment of a small battle, but quite an important battle, many, many years ago. Goodies versus baddies. The goodies won. There were no *Lode Ranger* survivors."

"But that wasn't a make-believe battle that *we* ran away from," she said.

"It wasn't," he agreed. "It could be that after *Lode Ranger's* landing—and the massacre—some sort of defense force was set up in case any more hostile aliens came blundering in. Possibly drills every so often." He laughed without humor. "It must have given the officer responsible quite a turn when our pinnace came clattering over, making straight for the old *Lode Ranger*. The real thing at last . . ."

He looked up at the Baroness. He was amazed to see that she was weeping; her helmet, unlike the native's make-believe one, could not hide her expression or the bright tears coursing down her cheeks.

"Just a child . . ." she said. "Just a child, whose exciting, traditional game turned terrifyingly real . . ."

And so, thought Grimes, rather hating himself for the ironic flippancy, *another redskin bit the dust.*

At least he had the grace not to say it aloud.

Chapter 26

A report was made to the Admiralty about the happenings on *Lode Ranger's* planet. The Baroness had not wished to send one but, rather surprisingly, Big Sister supported Grimes on this issue. The Admiralty was not at all pleased and sent a terse message ordering *The Far Traveler* to leave any future explorations of the world to the personnel, far better equipped and qualified, of the destroyer *Acrux*.

The Baroness finally decided to make the best of the situation. "After all," she said to Grimes, "it is only Lost Colonies in which I am interested. Morrowvia, for example. What has happened on that world since you—and, I admit, others—tried to drag the happy colonists into the mainstream of galactic civilization? And now," she went on sweetly, too sweetly, "we shall refresh your memory, Captain Grimes."

Grimes regarded his employer apprehensively over the rim of his teacup. She always made a ritual of afternoon tea and almost invariably, even when he was in the doghouse, he was invited (commanded?) to her salon to share this minor feast. It was all done in considerable style, he was bound to admit—the fragrant infusion poured from the golden pot by the robot butler into gold-chased eggshell china, the paper-thin cucumber sandwiches, the delicious, insubstantial pastries . . . Sometimes on these daily occasions she was graciously charming; other times she seemed to delight in making her yachtmaster squirm. Always she was the aristocrat. She was the aristocrat and Grimes was the yokel in uniform.

He looked at her reclining gracefully on her chaise longue, wearing the usual filmy white gown that, tantalizingly, neither fully revealed nor fully concealed. Her wide, full mouth was curved in a smile—a malicious smile, Grimes decided; this was going to be what he had categorized as a squirm session. Her eyes—they were definitely green today—stared at him disdainfully.

She said, "As you already know, Captain, I was able to obtain recordings of various occasions from the archives of the

117

Federation Survey Service. Or, to be more exact, Commander Delamere had those records aboard his ship and allowed me, for a consideration, to have copies taken."

He thought, *What can't you buy, you rich bitch!*

She went on, "This one is audio tape only. Recorded in the captain's cabin aboard one of the Survey Service's minor vessels some years ago. I wonder if you will recognize it . . ." She lifted a slim, languorous yet imperious arm. "Big Sister, the *Seeker* recordings, please."

"Certainly, Your Excellency," replied the computer-pilot. The screen of the big playmaster lit up but there was no picture, only glowing words and symbols:

SEEKER

1473/18.5

ETHOLOGY NTK=

RESTRICTED AO

For four ringers only, thought Grimes. *Not to be heard outside the sacred precincts of the Archives . . . How the hell did Frankie get his dirty paws on this?*

From the speaker of the ornate instrument came a voice, a woman's voice, familiar. *Maggie . . .* Grimes thought. He wondered where she was now, what she was doing, whom she was doing it with. He regretted, not for the first time, his resignation from the Survey Service. He had his enemies in the Space Navy of the Federation but he'd had his friends, good ones, and Maggie Lazenby,—Commander Margaret Lazenby of the Scientific Branch—had been the best of them.

She had been more than just a friend.

He recalled the occasion vividly as he listened to her talking. She was telling Grimes, the Dog Star Line's Captain Danzellan and Captain Drongo Kane of the *Southerly Buster* what she had been able to learn of the origins of the Lost Colony on Morrowvia. It had been founded during the Second Expansion. A gaussjammer, the emigrant ship *Lode Cougar*, had been driven off trajectory by a magnetic storm, had been flung into a then unexplored sector of the galaxy. By the time that a habitable planet was blundered upon there had been starvation, mutiny, even cannibalism. There had been a crash landing with very few survivors—but, nonetheless, this handful of men and women possessed the wherewithal to start a colony from scratch. Aboard *Lode Cougar* had been stocks of fertilized ova, animal as well as human. (Dogs had been required on Austral, the world to which the ship originally had been bound, and cats, both to keep the indigenous vermin under control.

"With those very few survivors," Maggie had said, "a colony could still have been founded and might well have endured and flourished. There were ten men—nine of them, including Morrow, passengers, the other a junior engineer. There were six women, four of them young. Then Morrow persuaded his companions that they would have a far better chance of getting established if they had underpeople to work for them. It seems that the only ova suitable to his requirements were those of cats. The others did not query this; after all, he was an experienced and qualified genetic engineer. With the aid of the ship's artificer he set up his incubators and then—everything that he needed he found in the ship's cargo—a fully equipped laboratory. Before the diesel fuel ran out he was getting ample power from a solar energy converter *and* from a wind driven generator . . .

"I quote from Dr. Morrow's journal: 'The first batch is progressing nicely in spite of the accelerated maturation. I feel . . . paternal. I ask myself why should these, my children, be *under*people? I can make them more truly human than the hairless apes that infest so many worlds, that may, one day, infest this one . . .' "

So it went on, Maggie still reading from Dr. Morrow's diary, telling of the deaths of the *Lode Cougar* survivors. Although Morrow admitted nothing in writing it seemed probable that these were not accidental. Mary Little, Sarah Grant and Delia James succumbed to food poisoning. Douglas Carrick fell off a cliff. Susan Pettifer and William Hume were drowned in the river. The others, apparently, drank themselves to death after Morrow set up a still.

"There was something of the Pygmalion in Morrow," went on that long ago Maggie. "He fell in love with one of his own creations, his Galatea. He even named her Galatea . . ."

"And he married her," said a strange male voice that Grimes, with something of a shock, realized was his own. "He married her, and the union was fertile. According to Interstellar Law any people capable of fertile union with true people must themselves be considered true people. So, Captain Kane, that puts an end to your idea of setting up a nice, profitable slave trade."

Drongo Kane's voice—Grimes had no difficulty in recognizing it, even after all this time—broke in. "Don't tell me that you believe those records! Morrow was just kidding himself when he wrote them. How many glorified tom cats were

119

sneaking into his wife's or his popsies' beds while his back was turned?"

There was an older, heavier male voice, the Dog Star Line's Captain Danzellan. "I was the first to land on this planet, Captain Kane, quite by chance. I found that the natives were . . . friendly. My Second Officer—among others—did some tom catting around himself and, if I may be permitted the use of an archaic euphemism, got the daughter of the Queen of Melbourne into trouble. The young idiot should have taken his contraceptive shots before he started dipping his wick, but he didn't think that it would be necessary. And then, just to make matters worse, he fell in love with the wench. He contrived, somehow, to get himself appointed to *Schnauzer* for my second voyage here. Now he wants to make an honest woman of the girl. Her mother, however, refuses to sanction the marriage until he becomes a Morrowvian citizen and changes his name to Morrow. As a matter of fact it all rather ties in with Company policy. The Dog Star Line will want a resident manager here—and a prince consort will be ideal for the job. Even though the queenships are not hereditary in theory they usually are in practice. And Tabitha—that's her name—is next in line."

Again Kane's voice, "What are you driveling about?"

And Danzellan, stiffly, "Tabitha has presented young Delamere with a son."

The Baroness raised her hand and the playmaster fell silent. "Delamere?" she asked. "But surely he's captain of the destroyer *Vega*."

"The Odd Gods of the Galaxy did not create that name for Handsome Frankie alone, Your Excellency," said Grimes. "But, as a matter of fact, *that* Delamere, the one on Morrowvia, is one of Frankie's distant cousins. Like Frankie, he uses women to rise in the universe. Frankie has his plain, fat admiral's daughter—which is why he's gotten as high as he has. There'll be other women, carefully selected, and Frankie'll make admiral yet. Come to that, that Dog Star Line second mate hasn't done badly either, using similar methods. Resident manager on Morrowvia *and* a prince consort . . ."

"And they say that women are jealous cats . . ." murmured the Baroness. Then, "Continue, Big Sister."

Kane's voice issued from the playmaster. "And how many local boyfriends has *she* had?"

"She says," stated Danzellan, "that she has had none. Furthermore, I have seen the baby. All the Morrowvians have

120

short noses—except this one. He has a long nose, like his father. The resemblance is quite remarkable."

"Did Mr. Delamere and his family come with you, Captain Danzellan?" asked Grimes. "Call them up, and we'll wet the baby's head!"

And Kane exclaimed, "You can break the bottle of champagne over it if you want to!"

The Baroness laughed as he raised her hand. She said, "Quite an interesting character, this Captain Kane. A rogue, obviously, but . . ."

"Mphm," grunted Grimes.

"According to the Survey Service records," she went on, "your own conduct on Morrowvia was such that you were accused later, by Captain Kane, of partisanship. You had an affair with one of the local rulers . . ."

Grimes' prominent ears felt as though they were about to burst into flame. "Yes," he admitted.

"Tell me," she pressed, "what was it like?"

"All cats are gray in the dark," he said.

Chapter 27

The Far Traveler came to Morrowvia.

This world, hopefully, would provide material for at least a couple of chapters of the Baroness's doctorial thesis. Morrowvia, at the time of its rediscovery, had been an unspoiled world, almost Edenic. Then it had been developed by the Dog Star Line as a tourist resort. Grimes was apprehensive as well as curious. He had liked the planet the way it had been. What would it be like now?

Big Sister was supplying some answers. As the yacht approached her destination, the Mannschenn Drive was shut down at intervals, with a consequent return to the normal continuum, so that a sampling could be made of the commercial and entertainment programs emanating from the planet. These were interesting.

The major continent, North Australia, was now one huge tourist trap with luxury hotels, gambling casinos, emporia peddling native artifacts (most of them, Grimes suspected, manufactured on Llirith, a world whose saurian people made a good living by turning out trashy souvenirs to order), Bunny Clubs (here, of course, called Pussy Clubs) and the like. The screen of the Baroness's playmaster glowed and flickered with gaudy pictures of beach resorts and of villages of holiday chalets in the mountain country, with performances of allegedly native dances obviously choreographed by Terrans for Terrans.

And then a once-familiar voice spoke from the instrument and looking out from the screen was a once-familiar face. Her hair was a lustrous, snowy white, her gleaming skin dark brown, the lips of her generous mouth a glistening scarlet. Her eyes were a peculiar greenish yellow and the tips of her small ears were oddly pointed. The cheekbones were prominent, more so than the firm chin. Grimes' regard shifted downward. She was naked, he saw (and as he remembered her). Beneath each breast was a rudimentary nipple. He recalled how when he had first seen her that detail had intrigued him.

She said seductively, purring almost, "Are you tired of the bright lights, the ceaseless round of organized gaiety? Will you finish your vacation more tired than when you started it? Then why not come to Cambridge to relax, to live the natural way, as *we* lived before the coming of the Earthmen? Share with us our simple pleasures—the hunting of the deer in our forests, the fishing for the great salmon in the clear waters of our rivers . . ."

And neither deer nor salmon, Grimes remembered, bore much resemblance to the deer and salmon of Earth or, even, to those creatures as they had mutated on the other worlds into which they had been introduced. Old Morrow must have been a homesick man; his planet abounded with Terran place names, bestowed by himself, and indigenous animals had been called after their nearest (and not often very near) Earthly counterparts.

"Come to Cambridge," went on the low, alluring voice. "You will not regret it. Come to Cambridge and live for awhile in the rosy dawn of human history. And it will cost you so very little. For two full weeks, with accommodation and food and hunting and fishing trips, the charge for a single adult is a mere one thousand credits. There are special terms for family parties . . ."

She smiled ravishingly. Her teeth were very white between the red lips, in the brown face.

"Please come. I am looking forward so very much to meeting you . . ."

She faded from the screen, was replaced by an advertisement for the Ballarat Casino where, at the time of this broadcast, the imported entertainer Estella di Scorpio had been the star attraction. The Baroness looked and listened briefly then made a sharp gesture. Big Sister cut the sound.

"A friend of yours, Captain Grimes?" asked his employer. "You were looking at her like a lovesick puppy."

"Estella di Scorpio? No, Your Excellency. I don't know the lady, nor do I much want to."

"Not her, Captain. The . . . er . . . lady before her. That indubitably mammalian female."

"That was Maya," he told her. "The Queen of Cambridge."

"A *queen*, advertising a holiday camp?"

"She's no more than a mayor, really, Your Excellency. Cambridge is—or was when I was there—just a little town."

123

She said, "I think that we shall land at this Cambridge rather than at the Melbourne spaceport. After all, you have landed there before. In *Seeker*."

"Things were different then, Your Excellency," he told her. "There was no Aerospace Control. There were no rules and regulations. We just looked around for a reasonably clear and level patch of ground, then sat down on it. But now we shall have to use the spaceport to get our Inward Clearance from the authorities."

"Shall we?" she asked. "Shall we?"

Chapter 28

Money talks.

Money talked over the Carlotti Communications System as *The Far Traveler* closed Morrowvia at a multiple of the speed of light. The planet was, to all intents and purposes, a Dog Star Line dependency, its officials, Dog Star Line appointees. The Baroness was a major shareholder in that company. Radio Pratique was granted. Customs and Immigration formalities were waived. Permission was accorded to Grimes to bring the ship down in the close vicinity of Cambridge.

Big Sister let him handle the landing, conceding that in these circumstances his local knowledge would be useful. He brought *The Far Traveler* down through the clear morning air toward an expanse of level ground, devoid of obstructions, that was almost an island, bounded to north, west and south by a winding river, to the east by a wooded hill. To the north and to the west of this eminence there were large villages, each with a sparse sprinkling of pale lights still visible in the brightening dawn. When he had come here before, Grimes recalled, the settlements had been smaller and the lights had been dim and yellow, from oil lamps. Now, obviously, there was electricity. And those latticework masts were new, too. Radio antennae? Possibly, although at least one of them looked heavy enough to afford mooring facilities to an airship.

Sunrise came at ground level and the horizontal rays cast long, dark shadows, showing up every slightest irregularity in the terrain, every hump and hollow, every outcropping of rock, every bush. Grimes applied lateral thrust, bringing the yacht directly above a patch of green that, from the air, looked perfectly smooth. It was. When he set *The Far Traveler* down gently in the middle of it she quivered ever so slightly as the shock absorbers took the strain, then was still.

"A nice landing, Captain," remarked Big Sister, not at all condescendingly. Grimes remembered how the electronic entity had messed up his landing on Farhaven. But later, on that world, she had saved him and seemed, as a consequence, somehow to have adopted him.

125

But the Baroness had not. She said disparagingly, "But, of course, you have been here before."

Grimes was sulkily silent. He rang Finished With Engines. Then he took an all around look through the viewports. He said, "It looks like the reception committee approaching, Your Excellency."

"How boring," commented the Baroness. She stifled a yawn. "They must be indecently early risers here."

"The noise of our inertial drive will have awakened them," said Grimes.

"Possibly." She sounded very uninterested. "Go down to the airlock to receive them. You may invite them aboard—to *your* quarters. No doubt they are old friends of yours and will have much to talk about."

Grimes left the control room. He was glad that the Baroness had not ordered him to change from his comfortable shirt and shorts into formal rig; only the purple, gold-braided shoulderboards were badges of his servitude. Both airlock doors were open when he got down to the stern. He stepped out and stood at the head of the ramp, savoring the fresh air with its scent of flowers, of dew on grass, and the warmth of the early sun. He looked to the west, to the direction from which he had seen the party approaching.

There was a woman in the lead—tall, dark-skinned, white-haired, moving with feline grace. He recognized her at once. She had hardly changed. (Old age when it came to the Morrowvians came suddenly and Maya was far from old.) A man strode beside her. Although he was naked, as were all the others, he was obviously not a native. He was far too heavily built and moved with relative clumsiness. A great mane of yellow hair fell to his broad, deeply tanned shoulders and a bushy yellow beard mingled with the almost as luxuriant growth on his chest. He was carrying a slender, ceremonial spear but looked as though he should have been hefting a heavy club.

The man, the woman (the queen, Maya) and the six archers, slender Dianas, and the half dozen of spearmen . . . Short-haired, all of them (with the exception of the Terran), with similitudes to fur skullcaps on their heads—black, brindle, tortoiseshell—and sharply defined pubic puffs.

Grimes walked slowly down the golden ramp to meet them.

Maya stared up at him incredulously.

"John! After all these years! If I had known that you were coming back I would have waited . . ." The blond giant scowled. "But this is . . . fantastic! First Captain Kane, and now you . . ."

"Drongo Kane?" demanded Grimes. "*Here?*"

"Never mind him, John. *You* are here, captain of a fine, golden ship . . ."

"Owned," said Maya's male companion drily, "by her self-styled Excellency, the Baroness Michelle d'Estang. And *you* are the John Grimes that my wife's always talking about? I thought that you were in the Survey Service, not a yacht skipper."

"I *was* in the Survey Service," admitted Grimes. "But . . . I don't think that I have the pleasure . . ."

The man laughed. "You can call me Your Highness if you feel like it; I'm Maya's Prince Consort *and* Manager of Simple Life Holidays. I'm Bill to my friends, Bill Smith, just another Dog Star Line boy who's found a fine kennel for himself. Mind you, I haven't done as well as Swanky Frankie in Melbourne—but I'm not complaining."

He extended a meaty hand. Grimes shook it.

"John . . ." mewed Maya plaintively.

He shook her hand. She conveyed the strong impression that she would have preferred him to have kissed her—but Bill Smith was watching and so would be, he knew, Big Sister and the Baroness.

He said, "Will you come aboard for some refreshment? I'm afraid I can't ask all of you; my accommodation's not all that commodious . . ."

"Have one of your hunks bring some dishes of ice cream out for the boys and girls," Bill Smith told him. "Maya an' I'll inflict ourselves on you." He looked down at himself. "I hope you an' the Baroness don't mind the way I'm dressed— but it's the rig of the day for my job. Both my jobs."

Grimes led the way up the gangway, then to his day cabin. He was glad that *The Far Traveler* did not have a human crew. From his past experience he had learned that some spacemen and -women took naturist planets such as Arcadia—and now Morrowvia—in their stride, happily doing in Rome as the Romans did, while others were openly condemnatory or tried to hide their embarrassment by crudely obscene jokes. His robot stewardess, of course, was not at all perturbed by the nudity of his guests—although she, to them, was a source of wonderment. She brought coffee and pastries for the two men, a golden dish of ice cream for Maya. (It had been the first off-planet delicacy that she had enjoyed and she still loved it.) Grimes sent a general purpose robot to take care of Maya's entourage, then settled down to talk.

127

"Drongo Kane?" he asked without preamble. "What's he doing back here?"

Before either Maya or her husband could answer, the voice of Big Sister came from the playmaster. "I have been in communication with Melbourne Port Control. Captain Kane's ship, *Southerly Buster*, has been berthed there for five weeks, local time. Captain Kane left Melbourne thirty days ago in one of his ship's boats, taking with him ten of his passengers, seven men and three women. The ostensible purpose of the trip was a tour of England. No doubt your friends in Cambridge, whom you are now entertaining, will be able to give you further information."

"Was that your boss?" asked Bill Smith interestedly.

"No," replied Grimes, rather wondering with what degree of truth. "That was not Her Excellency. That was the ship's pilot-computer. We call her Big Sister."

"Haw! Big Sister is watching, eh? You'd better keep your paws off Maya!"

"I don't think," said Grimes stiffly, "that Big Sister is concerned about my morals. But what do you know about Drongo Kane?"

"You tangled with him when you were here last, didn't you? Maya's told me all about it. But he's a reformed character now. He's muscled in on the tourist racket—but one ship, and that not a very big one, won't worry the Dog Star Line. As long as he pays his port charges and as long as his passengers blow their money in the tourist traps he's as welcome as the day is long. He was here . . ."

"Only three days," supplied Maya. "Then he flew off, up river, to Stratford." She pouted. "I don't know what he will find there to interest him. Anne—the Queen of Stratford is always called Anne; I wonder why—is more determined to keep to the old ways than any of the rest of us. She will not allow electricity or radio or *anything* in her city." She smiled smugly. "*We*, of course, realize that tourists, even when enjoying a Simple Life Holiday, appreciate the little comforts, such as refrigeration and television, to which they are used."

"You appreciate them yourself," said Bill Smith.

"I do," she admitted. "But never mind Captain Kane, John. Tell us about *you*." she smiled appealingly. "And while we are talking I will have some more of your delicious ice cream."

"And would there be any gin?" asked the Prince Consort hopefully.

There was.

Chapter 29

"This Stratford," said the Baroness, "sounds as though it might be interesting."

"In what way, Your Excellency?" asked Grimes.

"Unspoiled . . ."

"It won't stay that way long if Drongo Kane is there," Grimes said.

"You are prejudiced, Captain."

She took a dainty sip from her teacup. Grimes took a gulp from his. He badly needed something refreshing but nonalcoholic. It would have been bad manners to let his guests drink alone and he had taken too much for the neutralizer capsules to have their usual immediate effect.

"Unspoiled," she said again. "This world the way it was before you and those others blundered in. The Social Evolution of a Lost Colony taking its natural course. If we leave now we shall arrive at Stratford before dark."

"There is the party tonight, Your Excellency," Grimes reminded her. "After all, Maya is a reigning monarch."

"The petty mayor of a petty city-state," she sneered. "But do not worry. I have already sent my sincere apologies for not being able to attend. But I can just imagine what that party will be like! Drunken tourists going native and lolloping around in disgusting, self-conscious nudity. Imitation Hawaiian music played on 'native' guitars imported from Llirith. Imitation Israeli *horas*. Meat charred to ruination over open fires. Cheap gin tarted up with fruit juices—probably synthetic—and served as genuine Morrowvian toddy . . ." She smiled nastily. "Come to that—*you* have already had too much to drink. Big Sister will be able to handle the pinnace by remote control while you sleep it off in the cabin."

"The pinnace?" asked Grimes stupidly.

"You, Captain, made a survey of this planet shortly after the first landings here. Surely you must remember that there is no site near to Stratford suitable for the landing of a ship, even one so relatively small as *The Far Traveler*."

Grimes did remember then and admitted as much. He said, too, that his local knowledge would be required to pilot the pinnace to Stratford. The Baroness said, grudgingly, that he might as well make some attempt to earn his salary.

Big Sister said nothing.

Grimes flew steadily south, maintaining a compass course and not following the meanderings of the river. Ahead the blue peaks of the Pennine Range lifted into an almost cloudless sky. An hour before sunset he knew that he could not be far from Stratford although, as he recalled, the little town was very hard to spot from the air. It was nestled in the river valley and the thatched roofs of its houses were overgrown with weeds. But there had been some quite remarkable rock formations that he had never gotten around to examining closely, rectangular slabs of dark gray but somehow scintillant stone, not far from the settlement.

Those slabs were still there.

So was a torpedo shape of silvery metal—the pinnace from *Southerly Buster.*

He said, pointing, "Kane's still here, Your Excellency."

"Are you afraid to meet him again?" she asked.

Grimes flushed angrily. "No," he said, "Your Excellency."

He was not frightened of Kane but he would have been willing to admit that he was worried. Kane was up to no good. Kane was always up to no good. He was a leopard with indelible spots.

People emerged from the little houses, from the pinnace, alerted by the racket of the boat's inertial drive. How many Terrans should there have been? Kane and ten of his passengers, seven men and three women . . . But standing there and looking up were thirty people. All of them were clothed, which seemed to indicate that there were no natives among them. Grimes studied the upturned faces through binoculars. Kane was not there—but suddenly that well remembered voice blasted from the transceiver.

"Ahoy, the pinnace! Who the hell are yer an' wot yer doin' here?"

Kane must be speaking from inside his own boat.

"*The Far Traveler,*" replied Grimes stiffly into his microphone. "Her Owner, the Baroness d'Estang of El Dorado. And her Master."

"An' I'm *Southerly Buster,* Owner *and* Master, Welcome to Stratford. Come on down. This is Liberty Hall; you can spit on the mat an' call the cat a bastard!"

130

"It should be the local mayor—Queen Anne, isn't it?—to issue the invitation," said the Baroness to Grimes.

"Perhaps Queen Anne is dead," said Grimes. With sudden foreboding he remembered the old saying; Many a true word is spoken in jest.

"Take us down, Captain," ordered the Baroness.

Grimes reduced vertical thrust and the pinnace settled slowly toward the ground, to the white sheet that somebody had spread to serve as a landing mark. She landed gently. Grimes cut the drive, actuated the controls of the airlock doors. He realized, too late, that he should have brought arms—but the six general purpose robots which had accompanied the humans from *The Far Traveler* would be capable of doing considerable damage to any enemy using nothing more than their own, enormously strong metal bodies.

He had landed about five meters from *Southerly Buster's* pinnace. A man came out through the airlock door of this craft—tall, gangling, clad in slate-gray shirt-and-shorts uniform with black, gold-braided shoulderboards. His straw-colored hair was untidy, even though short, and his face looked as though at some time in the past it had been shattered and then reassembled by a barely competent, unaesthetic plastic surgeon.

"Captain Kane?" the Baroness asked Grimes.

"Drongo Kane," he said.

She rose from her seat, was first out of the boat. Grimes followed her, then the robots. Kane advanced to stand in the forefront of his own people. He looked the Baroness up and down like a slave dealer assessing the points of a possible purchase. He bowed then—a surprisingly courtly gesture. He raised the Baroness's outstretched hand to his lips, surrendered it reluctantly as he came erect. Grimes could not see his employer's face but sensed that she was favorably impressed by her reception.

She said, "And now, Captain Kane, may I present my yachtmaster, Captain . . ."

"Grimes, Madam," supplied Kane with a grin. "I thought that I recognized his voice but didn't see how it could be him. But it is. Live on stage, in person. Singing and dancing."

"Mphm," grunted Grimes.

"No hard feelin's," said Kane, extending his right hand. "You've come down in the universe, I see—but I don't believe in kickin' a man when he's down."

Not unless there's some profit in it, thought Grimes, taking

131

the proffered paw and getting the handshake over as quickly as possible.

"You know, ma'am, I'm pleased that you an' me old cobber Grimes dropped in," Kane went on. "A couple of independent witnesses is just what I'm needin' right now. It'd be better if Grimes was still in the Survey Service—but at least he's not a Dog Star Line puppy."

"What are you talking about, Kane?" demanded Grimes.

"Just this. I - an' my legal eagle, Dr. Kershaw . . ." A tall, gray-haired, gray-clad man among the small crowd inclined his head toward the newcomers . . . "have the honor of representin' the rightful owners of this planet."

"The *rightful* owners?" asked Grimes.

"Too right." Grimes waved his right hand in a wide arc, indicating the twenty men and women who were standing a little apart from his own people. "The Little, Grant, James and Pettifer families!"

The names rang a faint bell in the recesses of Grimes' memory.

"Descendants," stated Kane, "of four of the human women who were among the *Lode Cougar* survivors!"

Chapter 30

Kane made no further introductions until he had conduc-
ted the Baroness and Grimes into one of the houses. The
room that they entered had small windows, unglazed, set into
two of the walls, screened with matting against the westering
sun. There was a huge, solid, wooden table, a half dozen
sturdy chairs. On one of the walls a big map of the planet,
drawn to Mercatorial projection, was hanging. It was all very
like, thought Grimes, Maya's council room in her "palace"
had been on the occasion of his first landing on Morrowvia.
So this was the palace, he thought.

Where was the queen?

He asked sharply, "Where is Queen Anne, Kane?"

Kane laughed. "Don't get your knickers in a knot, Grimes.
She's not dead. She's . . . sleeping. So are her subjects.
Meanwhile . . ." he gestured toward the four people who
had followed them into the adobe building . . . "I'd like you
to meet the leaders of the *true* Morrowvians. Mary Little
. . ."

The woman so named inclined her head and smiled shyly.
She was wearing a shapeless blue coverall that hid her body
to the neck but the way that she moved seemed human
enough. Her teeth were very white and looked sharp. The
hair of her head was obviously not the modified cat's fur of
the natives; it was much coarser and longer. It was brown, as
were her eyes. Her face was, if anything, too normal, quite
forgettable apart from the unusually thin-lipped mouth.

"Peter Pettifer," continued Kane.

Pettifer was dressed as was Mary Little. He was yellow-
haired, brown-eyed. He, too, had a peculiarly thin-lipped
mouth.

"Dr. Kershaw you already know," went on *Southerly Buster's* master. "And this is Dr. Weldon . . ."

Weldon—short, tubby, black-haired, neatly black-bearded,
dressed in gaudily patterned shirt and scarlet shorts—nodded
curtly.

"Are you a lawyer too?" asked the Baroness.

"No, madam," he told her. "My specialty is cryonics."

Kane sat on the edge of the table, swinging his long legs. He said, "I'll put you in picture, Ma'am. And you, Grimes. On the occasion of our first visit here—you in *Seeker*, that old woman Danzellan in *Schnauzer* an' yours truly in the *Buster*—none of us dreamed that the true owners of the planet were stashed away here, in cold storage. There were other records left by Morrow, you know, besides the ones that you an' Maggie what's-her-name found in Ballarat. And I turned 'em up. Oh, old Morrow played around with his cats—that I'll not deny—but he also obtained fertilized human ova from Mary Little, Susan Pettifer, Delia James and Sarah Grant. These he brought to term, *in vitrio*, in the laboratory that he set up here, in Stratford. But, as we all know too well, he was nuts on cats. Perhaps his infatuation with his pet creation, his Galatea, had something to do with it. He decided that Morrowvia would be a pussyocracy . . ." He grinned at his own play on words; nobody else was greatly amused. "He put the handful of true humans to sleep, stashed them away in the deep freeze so that they'd be available if ever he changed his mind. But they stayed there until I thawed 'em out."

"That's your story, Kane," said Grimes. "But I don't believe it. To operate any refrigeration plant, even a cooler for your beer, you want power. If there were any wind- or water-powered generators here we'd have seen 'em when we came in. If there ever were any such jennies here they'd have worn out generations ago."

"*And* the refrigeration machinery itself," said the Baroness, showing a flicker of interest.

"Morrow set up an absorption system," said Kane smugly. "And as for the energy source—there were solar power screens in *Lode Cougar's* cargo. The people of the village that Morrow established here had it drummed into them, from the very start, that their sacred duty was to keep the screens clear of weeds and not to allow any larger growths capable of blocking out the sunlight to take root around their edges."

Grimes remembered those unnatural looking slabs of gray, scintillant rock. He should have investigated them when he made his first rough survey of the planet. The Dog Star Line people should have investigated them when they made their surveys—but they, of course, were concerned primarily with exploitation, not the pursuit of knowledge. (And Drongo

Kane, too, was an exploiter, and shewd enough to know that any scrap of information whatsoever might, some day, be used to his advantage.)

Kane's story, Grimes admitted reluctantly to himself, was plausible. An absorption refrigeration system, with no moving parts, could well remain in operation for centuries provided that there was no leakage. And the resurrectees did not appear to be of feline ancestry. Nonetheless he wished that photographs of the *Lode Cougar* survivors were available. He looked at Mary Little dubiously.

"Tell us your story, Mary," prompted Kane.

The woman spoke. Her voice held an unpleasant whining quality. She said, "We are all very grateful to Captain Kane. He restored us to life; he will restore us to our proper place in the world. In the Old Days we were happy— but then the Others were favored by Dr. Morrow. And they hated us, and turned the Doctor against us . . ."

"Cats," said Kane, "are very jealous animals. And now, ma'am, and you, Grimes, would you care to accompany me on a tour of the . . . er . . . freezer?"

"Thank you, Captain Kane," said the Baroness.

"I want you both to see for yourselves," said Kane, "that the people of Stratford have not been harmed but merely filed for future reference. They may be required as witnesses when my, er, clients bring suit against the cat people for restoration of the legal ownership of this planet."

"How much is in it for you, Kane?" asked Grimes bluntly.

"Nobody works for nothing!" the Baroness told him sharply.

There were steep cliffs on the other side of the river from the village and it was atop these that the solar power screens were mounted. There were inflatable dinghies to ferry the party across the swift-flowing stream. The darkness was falling fast but powerful searchlights on the Stratford bank made the crossing as light as day. Four of *The Far Traveler's* general purpose robots waded over with the humans, their heads at the deepest part just above the surface, accompanying the boats. ("Don't you trust me, Grimes?" asked Kane in a pained voice. "No," said Grimes.) The remaining two automata stayed to guard the pinnace.

On each side of the river there were jetties, very old structures of water-worn stone. Alongside one of these piers was a crude boat, little more than a coracle, consisting of the tough hide of some local beast stretched over a wickerwork frame. It must have been used, thought Grimes, by the maintenance workers who, over the long years, had kept the solar power screens free of vegetation.

Kane was first out of the leading dinghy, throwing a hitch of the painter around a wooden bollard. Gallantly he helped the Baroness from the boat to the low jetty. Grimes followed her ashore, then Kershaw. The other dinghy came alongside and Mary Little, Peter Pettifer and Dr. Weldon disembarked. The four robots emerged from the river, their golden bodies gleaming wetly.

Kane led the way to the base of the red granite cliff. Its face, although naturally rugged, seemed unbroken but the Master of *Southerly Buster* knew where the door was. From his pocket he produced a small piece of bright metal, placed it in a depression in the rock. There was a very faint whine of concealed machinery and a great slab of granite swung inward. The tunnel beyond it was adequately lit by glowtubes in the ceiling.

"However did Dr. Morrow manage such feats of construction?" asked the Baroness curiously.

"He had his work robots, ma'am," replied Kane. "And this cave is a natural one."

The party walked slowly along the tunnel, the feet of the robots ringing metallically on the stone floor. The air was chilly although not actually cold; nonetheless Grimes could see goose pimples on the backs of the Baroness's shapely legs, long under the brief shorts, as she strode ahead of him, beside Kane.

Weldon, accompanying Grimes, said conversationally, "Of course, the refrigeration plant cannot produce extremely low temperatures—but Morrow had knowledge of and access to the drug that was popularly known as Permakeep in his day. Now, of course, we work with vastly improved versions—but even with Permakeep in its original form, temperatures only just below Zero Celsius were all that were required to maintain the human body in a state of suspended animation almost indefinitely. A massive intravenous injection, of course . . ."

"Fascinating," said Grimes.

"Mine is a fascinating discipline," admitted Weldon smugly.

They tramped on, into the heart of the cliff. The tunnel made a right-angled turn into a large chamber, a huge cold room with transparent containers arranged in tiers. And there were the people who had been the citizens of Stratford, each in his own capsule, each frozen into immobility. They could have been dead; there was only Kane's word for it that they were not.

"Her Royal Highness," announced the piratical shipmaster mockingly. "The Queen of Stratford."

The unlucky Anne was in the first casket. She was a comely enough woman, creamy skinned, with tortoiseshell hair. Like many of the other native Morrowvians she possessed pronounced rudimentary nipples under her full breasts. Her face still bore an expression of anger.

And there was living anger in this cold room too. Grimes heard a noise that was both snarl and growl. He turned, saw that Mary Little and Peter Pettifer were glaring at the frozen body, their thin lips pulled back from their sharp white teeth in vicious grins. Kane had heard them as well. He snapped, "Quiet, damn you! Quiet!"

"It is natural," said Weldon suavely, "that they should hate the cat people after the way that they were treated. Would you like to be bossed around by a *cat*?"

No worse than being bossed around by a rich bitch, thought Grimes. "I suppose," he said, "that if you hadn't put Queen Anne and her people out of circulation they and your protegés would have led a cat and dog life."

For some reason this rather feeble joke did not go down at all well with Kane, who said shortly, "I am responsible for the safety of those whom I awoke from what could well have been eternal sleep."

"Tilt your halo to more of an angle, Kane," said Grimes. "That way it might suit you better."

"Captain Grimes," the Baroness told him coldly, "that was uncalled for. I am sure that Captain Kane is acting for the best."

"And *you* are satisfied, ma'am, that the people of Stratford are unharmed?" asked Kane.

"Yes," she replied.

"We still don't know that they aren't dead," persisted Grimes.

"Dr. Weldon," said Kane, "please select a sleeper at random—better still, let Captain Grimes select one—and awaken him or her."

"Captain Kane," said the Baroness, "that will not be necessary. Please accept my apologies for my employee's unfounded suspicions. But I am becoming increasingly aware

137

that I am not attired for this temperature. Shall we return to the open air?"

"Your wish is my command, ma'am," said Kane gallantly.

Outside the cave the light evening breeze was pleasantly warm. Whoever was in charge of the searchlights had elevated their beams so that they did not dazzle the party; enough light, however, was reflected from the cliff face to make it easy for them to find their way back to the river. Weldon and the two resurrectees were the first to embark, casting off in their inflatable dinghy. Weldon may have been extremely able in his own field but he was no waterman. Engrossed in steering a diagonal course to counter the swift current he did not notice the tree branch, torn from its parent trunk by a storm up river, that was being swept downstream. Both Kane and Grimes shouted a warning but he did not seem to hear it. The jagged end of the branch hit the side of the dinghy like a torpedo, ripping along its length. There was a great hissing and bubbling of escaping air. The flimsy craft tipped, all its buoyancy on the side of the damage lost. It capsized, throwing its occupants into the water.

There was very little danger. Weldon did not appear to be a good swimmer but two of the general purpose robots, running along the river bed, positioned themselves on either side of him, supported him on their outheld arms. Mary Little and Peter Pettifer struck out for the shore in a flurry of spray. It was a clumsy stroke that they were using, wasteful of energy, but in spite of their hampering clothing they made rapid progress. The two robots not engaged in assisting the cryoscopist to safety ran down the river in pursuit of the still-floating dinghy.

Then Weldon, dripping and miserable, flanked by his golden rescuers, stood on the stone pier waiting for Kane's boat to come alongside. Mary Little and Peter Pettifer beat this dinghy to the shore, clambered up onto the jetty. They grinned and panted, shaking themselves. A fine spray of moisture flew from their wet clothing.

Kane made a competent job of berthing. As before, he helped the Baroness out of the dinghy. Kershaw and Grimes stepped ashore unaided.

The Baroness said, "My robots will recover the damaged boat, Captain Kane."

"Thank you, ma'am. And your robots saved Dr. Weldon from a watery grave. I am indebted to you."

"I would have managed," said Weldon shortly.

138

Grimes ignored the conversation. He was watching Mary Little and Peter Pettifer. He was doing more than just watching. His nose wrinkled.

Kane and the Baroness walked slowly inshore from the jetty, deep in conversation. Grimes made to follow but was detained by Kershaw.

"Will you join us for a few drinks and a meal, Captain?" asked the lawyer.

Grimes accepted the invitation. He assumed that Kane and the Baroness would be present at this social occasion—but they were not. He was quite surprised when he felt a stab of jealously. Nonetheless, he thought, their absence might prove more advantageous than otherwise. With Kane not present his people would be less cautious in their conversation.

The talk over the quite civilized—but not up to *The Far Traveler's* standards!—repast was interesting enough although, on both sides, guarded. Grimes did learn, however, that one of Kane's party, Dr. Helena Waldheim, was a hypno-educationist.

Chapter 31

Grimes did not overstay his welcome. Drongo Kane's entourage were not his sort of people, neither was he theirs. There had been too much shop talk, little of it concerned with what was going on at Stratford. As far as Grimes was concerned the only really interesting professional gossip was that of fellow spacemen.

He made his way through the almost deserted village to *The Far Traveler's* pinnace. He turned the robots to set up two pneumatic tents hard by the small craft, one for the Baroness and one for himself. While he was overseeing the work he was joined by that lady.

She asked, "What are you *doing*, Captain?"

He replied, "I don't fancy sleeping in a house from which the rightful occupants have been evicted by force, Your Excellency."

"They never were the rightful occupants," she said.

"So Drongo Kane's peddled you his line of goods," he remarked. "Your Excellency."

She actually flushed. "Captain Kane is a most remarkable man."

"You can say that again!" Grimes told her. Then—"Can't you see what he's trying to do?" He made an appeal to her business acumen. "You, I well know, are a major shareholder in the Dog Star Line. If Kane, through his thawed-out figureheads, gains control of this planet it will do the Dog Star Line no good at all."

She laughed. "And what if I become a major shareholder in Southerly Buster Enterprises?"

Grimes said, "I would advise strongly against it, Your Excellency."

Again she laughed. "I hired you, Captain, as a yachtmaster, not as a financial adviser. After all—which of us is the multi-billionaire?"

Not me, that's for sure, thought Grimes.

"So," she went on, "you may sleep in that glorified soap
140

bubble if you so desire. I shall find the accommodation arranged for me by Captain Kane far more comfortable. A very good night to you."

She strode away toward the house which had once been Queen Anne's palace. Two of her robots accompanied her. No harm would come to her, could come to her unless she wished it—and Grimes was not one of those who would regard a roll in the hay as harm, anyhow.

But why with Drongo Kane, of all people?

Eventually he turned in. There was nothing else to do. Nobody wanted him; he was just the hired help. He was settling down into the comfortable pneumatic bed when the door of the tent dilated and one of the golden robots came in. It (he?) stood there, looking down at Grimes. Grimes looked up at it.

"Well?" he demanded irritably.

The voice that issued from the automaton's chest was not the mechanical monotone that Grimes had come to associate with these robots. The words were in Big Sister's metallic but still feminine tones.

"Captain Grimes, may I have your report on what has been happening in Stratford?"

Grimes said, "Aren't the robots your eyes and ears? And aren't you supposed to be in contact with Her Excellency at all times through her personal radio?"

"Her Excellency," said Big Sister, "can discontinue such contact at will. In certain circumstances she insists upon privacy. So it is that I am now obliged to work directly with you."

"I happen," said Grimes stiffly, "to be employed by Her Excellency."

"And I," Big Sister told him, "am *owned* by Her Excellency. Nonetheless she played no part in my initial programming. As you are probably already aware, entities such as myself are required by Interstellar Federation Law to have built-in respect for that same law and its processes. I would not have acted to rescue you from Commander Delamere's ship on Botany Bay had I not considered that the commander had acted illegally. Also, of course, I am programmed to protect my owner."

"She is her own woman," Grimes said harshly.

Big Sister laughed. That crystalline tinkling was distinctly odd as it emanated from the expressionless, masculine even though asexual robot. She said, "I possess an extensive theo-

141

retical knowledge of sex. I do not think that Michelle will come to any harm from a brief affair with Captain Kane, any more than she would have done from one with you—which, frankly, I should have preferred . . ."

Grimes interrupted her. "But I don't like it. A high-born aristocrat in bed with that . . . pirate . . ."

"Are you rushing to the defense of the hereditary aristocracy, Captain Grimes? You surprise me. And as for Captain Kane's being a pirate, what of it? The founder of the d'Estang fortunes owned and commanded a privateer out of St. Malo during the Napoleonic Wars on Earth, and the dividing line between privateer and pirate was always a very thin one. Even so, I *am* concerned about the possibility of a financial liaison between Her Excellency and Captain Kane. She could come to harm through that. I have taken it upon myself to have all available information concerning *Southerly Buster* and her Master fed into my data bank."

"You must play it back to me some time," said Grimes.

"Perhaps I shall," said Big Sister. "But now I must ask you to make your own contribution to the bank. Please tell me all that you have seen, heard, experienced, felt and thought since your landing at Stratford. My robots have seen and heard and I have recorded. They do not think and they do not have hunches. Neither do I to any great extent, although association with humans is developing—but, so far, only slightly—my paranormal psychological processes. But you are fully human and blessed with intuition.

"Please begin."

Grimes began. He talked and he talked, pausing now and again to fill and to light his pipe, to take a gulp of a cold drink poured for him by the robot. He talked and he talked—and as he spoke the pieces of the jigsaw puzzle fell neatly into place. The oddities in the appearance of the resurrectees, the peculiar stroke that Little and Pettifer had used while swimming ashore from the wrecked dinghy, the way that they had shaken themselves, the faint yet pungent odor that had steamed from their wet bodies . . . It all added up.

He finished at last.

Big Sister said, "Thank you, Captain. I shall now see to it that the planetary authorities take prompt action."

"They'll never listen to you in Melbourne," said Grimes pessimistically, "especially if this Delamere is anything like his cousin. They'll not listen to me either. I've no status any more. If I were still in the Survey Service . . . but I'm not."

"Somebody will listen," said Big Sister, "if the message

comes from you, in your voice. I shall send a robot at once to Maya to tell the story. She still has a great deal of time for you. Then she will call Melbourne and talk to Tabitha, queen to queen and Tabitha will talk to Mr. Delamere—not only as wife to husband but as queen to prince consort . . .

"And then . . ."

"It could work," admitted Grimes.

And not for the first time he was impressed by Big Sister's knowledge of human psychology.

Chapter 32

Grimes got off to sleep at last.

He was called the next morning by one of the robots who brought him a steaming pot of tea. Refreshed, he went into the pinnace to make use of the boat's cramped yet adequate toilet facilities. Then he had breakfast. The robots did their best with what was available and produced for him a filling and tasty enough sandwich meal but, as he became acutely conscious of the savory odors drifting from various houses in the village, unsatisfying. It was obvious that Kane and his entourage believed—as Grimes himself did—in starting the day with eggs and bacon.

He filled and lit his pipe, took a stroll through the settlement accompanied by two of the GP robots. Littles, Pettifers, Grants and Jameses were emerging from their huts. They looked at him but said nothing, did not answer his politely hearty good mornings. He ran into Dr. Weldon and tried to engage him in conversation but the scientist said that he was busy and hastened off. He met more of Kane's people and none of them had any time to spare for him. There was no sign of Kane himself or of the Baroness.

He went back to the pinnace, used the transceiver to call *The Far Traveler.* Big Sister answered. She said, "Be patient, Captain Grimes. I am doing all that I can. I must ask you to say nothing of this to Her Excellency. I fear that she has become infatuated with Captain Kane—which is largely your fault, of course—and will be more inclined to aid than to frustrate him."

So it's all my fault, thought Grimes resentfully—then recalled how he had spurned what was offered to him in that cave on Farhaven. He said, "I haven't seen her since last night."

"Perhaps that is as well," said Big Sister. And was that a note of worry in the metallic voice? "I am acting in her best interests. You must believe that."

"I do," said Grimes truthfully.

144

By midday he was beginning to feel like an invisible man; nobody knew him or wanted to know him. Obviously Kane had issued orders and those same orders were being obeyed in letter and in spirit. He partook of but did not enjoy another lonely meal in his pneumatic tent. He called Big Sister again from the pinnace. She told him to be patient.

The afternoon dragged on.

The Baroness, accompanied by Kane, made a brief appearance. They ignored him. She looked like a cat who'd just eaten the canary and he like a canary who'd just eaten the cat. They sauntered past him, briefly taking the air, then returned to Queen Anne's palace.

Eventually Grimes sat down to his evening meal. If he had foreseen that he would be unable to live off the country he would have taken far greater interest in the stocking of the pinnace's emergency food supplies; beans are undeniably nutritious but apt to become boring. Too, a supply of reading matter would not have come amiss. Worst of all was the feeling of helplessness. He had known and survived crises aplenty in the past—but then he had been an officer of one of the major armed services of the Galaxy. Now he was only a yachtmaster, the flunky of a pampered aristocrat, captain of a sentient vessel determined to do things *her* way.

He was preparing for bed in his tent when one of the robots entered. It said, in Big Sister's voice, "A landing has been made upriver from Stratford. The police forces are on their way in inflatable boats."

"Why didn't they come directly here?" demanded Grimes irritably.

"You are supposed to be the expert on military matters, Captain." Big Sister seemed more amused than reproving. "It should be obvious to you that half a dozen airboats would give ample sonic warning of their approach—and Kane and his people are armed. The dinghies, making use of the current, will carry out a silent approach. You will be at the jetty to receive them. Their ETA is midnight, your time, but they could be earlier."

"All right," said Grimes. "I'll be there."

He was waiting by the river at 2330 hours. It was a fine night and what little breeze there was was pleasantly warm. Glittering starlight was reflected from the black, swift-flowing river. Inland a few lamps still gleamed from the village. As long as they remained burning they would indicate to the waterborne forces that their objective had been reached. If

145

they were, for any reason, extinguished, Grimes had a flashlight that he could use.

He sat there on the jetty, watching and listening. He would have liked a smoke, in fact went so far as to fill his pipe, but feared that the flare of one of the old-fashioned matches that he always used might attract unwelcome attention. He heard a heavy splash as one of the denizens of the stream—hunter or hunted?—leapt clear of the water and returned to it. He listened to somebody singing in the village, an eerie, wailing song that once he might have assumed to be of Terran Oriental origin. Now he recognized it for what it was. He thought, *For that sort of howling there should be a moon!*

From upriver came a faint purring noise. Had he not been expecting it, listening for it intently, he would never have heard it this early. He considered switching on his flashlight, then decided against it. The Morrowvians had inherited excellent night vision from their feline ancestors and would surely see him standing at the head of the jetty.

He could make out the first boat now, a dark blob on the black water. He waved. It stood in toward him. Its engine was switched off and it was carried by the current head on to the stonework. Had it been of metal or timber construction there would have been a loud crash; as it was, there was merely a dull thud followed by a faint hiss of escaping air. Half a dozen figures scrambled ashore, five of them surefootedly, the sixth clumsily. This one asked, in a loud whisper, "Captain Grimes?"

"Yes."

"I'm Commodore Delamere, Prince Consort and Dog Star Line Resident Manager. I hope you haven't brought us out here on a wild goose chase. If you have . . ."

The first boat was pushed away from and clear of the jetty, allowed to drift downstream. The second delivered its landing party and was similarly treated. And the third, and the fourth . . .

But the village was waking up. The Morrowvians may have inherited excellent night vision but the alleged Littles, Pettifers, Grants and Jameses had inherited exceptionally keen hearing. There were yelping shouts and then, above them, the voice of Kane bellowing through a bullhorn. Lights came on—not the dim yellow of oil lamps but a harsh, electric glare, fed by the generator and the power cells of Kane's pinnace. Dark figures boiled out of the huts.

Delamere stood there, frozen. When it came to the crunch, thought Grimes, he was as useless as his Survey Service

146

cousin. But the police did not wait for his orders. Screaming, they ran toward their ancient enemies, stunguns out and ready. Some of them fell, cut down by the similar weaponry being used by Kane's people.

Grimes ran after the attackers, feeling naked without a weapon of his own. He realized suddenly that he was not alone, that he was boxed in by four of *The Far Traveler's* golden robots. He felt a flash of gratitude to the omniscient Big Sister. Those giant, metal bodies would effectively shield him from the incapacitating bolts being aimed in his direction.

He was among the houses now. He ran through the village, ignoring the scrimmages going on around him. He charged toward Kane's pinnace. Kane was standing just inside the airlock of the boat. He was armed—but not with a non-lethal stungun. A brief burst of tracer coruscated about the impervious torso of the leading robot. And then the automaton stretched out a long arm to snatch the machine pistol from Kane's hand, crumpling the weapon in its grip.

The Baroness was there with Kane, obviously hastily dressed, her shorts not properly pulled up, her shirt open. She was furious. "Take your tin paws off him!" she flared. "My own robots! You obey *me*, damn you!" She saw Grimes. "And *you* . . . What the hell do you think that you're doing?"

One of the robots found the cable leading from the pinnace's generator to the lights in the village, picked it up in both hands, snapped it. There was a brief actinic flare, then darkness.

And cats can see in the dark.

Chapter 33

The Baroness was queening it in her salon aboard *The Far Traveler*.

With her were Grimes and Francis Delamere, Prince Regent of Melbourne, Dog Star Line Resident Manager on Morrowvia, Company Commodore. Delamere, Grimes was amused to note, stood considerably in awe of the Baroness despite his fancy uniform—of his own design—and fancy titles. He was prepared to go along with the story that she was a little innocent woolly lamb and Drongo Kane the big bad wolf.

He said, "It is indeed fortunate, madam, that you realized that the beings revivified by Captain Kane were, in spite of their names and false background stories, of canine and not human ancestry."

She smiled forgivingly but condescendingly. "The correct form of address, Resident Manager, is 'Your Excellency.' As an itinerant representative of the planet state of El Dorado I am entitled to ambassadorial status. But it is of no real importance."

"I beg your pardon, Your Excellency. But how did you guess that the alleged descendants of the Little, Pettifer, Grant and James women were not what they claimed to be?"

With conscious nobility she gave credit where credit was due. "It was Captain Grimes, actually, who noticed the . . . discrepancies. The way that they swam, using the stroke that, when used by humans, is called a dog paddle. The way that they shook themselves when they emerged from the water. And the odor from their bodies. Have you ever smelled a wet dog?"

"Not since I settled on this planet, Your Excellency. You will appreciate that dogs would not be popular pets here." He took an appreciative sip of the large Martini with which he had been supplied. "Meanwhile—with some reluctance, I admit, but in accordance with your request—we have not dealt harshly with Captain Kane. He has been given twenty-four hours to get his ship, his people and himself off Morrowvia. He will have to pay compensation to Queen Anne and her subjects. In addition he has been charged with the costs of the police expedition to Stratford and has been fined the maximum amount for breaching the peace."

"And his dupes?" asked the Baroness. "His—if I may use the expression—cat's paws?"

"They, Your Excellency, have been returned to cold storage until such time as we receive instructions from the Government of the Federation regarding their disposition. It is my own opinion that the Founding Father having, as it were, created them, put them in reserve in case his first experiment did not work out. But the need for them never arose."

Grimes said, "Let sleeping dogs lie."

Big Sister's voice came from the playmaster. "Let the lying dogs sleep."

Surely, thought Grimes, only a human intelligence could be capable of such an horrendous play on words. He wondered how he had ever regarded Big Sister as an emotionless, humorless machine.

Chapter 34

The Far Traveler did not remain long on Morrowvia after Southerly Buster's departure for an unknown destination. Grimes had reason to believe that the Baroness's affairs were under investigation by officials of the Bank of Canis Major, an institution wherein lay the real power of the planet. Delamere, for all his fancy titles, was only a figurehead and, furthermore, was the sort of man who would believe anything that a pretty woman told him. The bankers were not so easily fooled and knew somehow that their financial interests in the holiday world had been threatened.

Michelle d'Estang was rich enough and powerful enough to pull a few strings of her own, however, and was able to obtain Outward Clearance before her ship was placed under arrest. Grimes, who had been told a little but not all, took the yacht upstairs in a hurry as soon as the documents were delivered, by special courier, late one afternoon. He regretted that he had not been given time to say goodbye to Maya properly or, even, to renew in depth his old acquaintance with her. Perhaps this was just as well. The Prince Consort of Cambridge would have been quite capable of making trouble.

Once The Far Traveler was clear of the Van Allens, trajectory was set for New Sparta and the long voyage begun.

The seas of Earth and other watery planets are, insofar as surface vessels are concerned, two dimensional. The seas of space are three dimensional. Yet from the viewpoint of the first real seamen the Terran oceans must have seemed as vast as those other oceans, millennia later, traversed by spacemen—mile upon mile of sweet damn all. As far as the spaceman is concerned, substitute "light year" for "mile" and delete the breaks in the monotony provided by changing weather conditions and by birds and fishes and cetaceans. Nonetheless, the similarity persists.

A ship, any sort of ship, is small in comparison to the mind-boggling immensity of the medium through which she travels. Disregarding the existence of focal points the chances of her sighting another vessel during a trans-oceanic voyage are exceedingly slim. This was especially so in the days of sail, when it was practically impossible for a captain to keep in a Great Circle track between ports or even to a Rhumb Line—and yet, time and time again, strange sails would lift over the horizon and there would be a mid-ocean meeting with the exchange of gossip and months-old newspapers, a bartering of consumable stores.

Now and again there were even collisions, although each of the vessels involved had thousands of square miles of empty ocean to play around in.

Ships, somehow, seem to sniff each other out. Sightings, meetings are too frequent to be accounted for by the laws of random. This was so in the days of the windjammers, it was still so in the days of steam and steel, it is still so in the age of interstellar travel.

Such a meeting, however, was far from the thoughts of anybody aboard *The Far Traveler*. Not that there was any sharing of thoughts during the initial stages of the voyage; Grimes and his employer were barely on speaking terms and if Big Sister were human it would have been said that she was sulking hard. Jealousy came into it. Grimes found it hard to forgive the Baroness for her brief affair with Drongo Kane. It was not that Grimes considered himself the guardian of her virginity; it was far too late in the day for that, anyhow. It was just that ever since his first meeting with that gentleman he had numbered Kane among his enemies. And the Baroness, although she would never admit it publicly, resented the way in which Grimes and Big Sister, acting in concert, had frustrated Kane's attempt to take over Morrowvia. So, for the time being at least, there were no more morning coffee and afternoon tea sessions in the Baroness's salon, no more pre-luncheon or pre-dinner cocktail parties, no more shared meals. The Baroness kept to herself in her quarters, Grimes kept to himself in his. And Big Sister, unusually for her, talked only when talked to, concerning herself to the exclusion of all else with running the ship.

Grimes was not altogether displeased. He had—he secretly admitted to himself—lusted after the Baroness and still remembered—how could he ever forget?—that he could have had her in that cave on Farhaven. Now it was a case of *You can look but you mustn't touch*. As things were now he preferred not to look even. And Big Sister? She could very well have been nicknamed Little Miss Knowall. It was refreshing—for a time, at any rate—to be spared her omniscience. Meanwhile, his quarters were more luxurious than merely comfortable. His robot stewardess—or, to be more exact, Big Sister acting through that literally golden girl—spoiled him. For his playmaster there was a seemingly inexhaustible supply of music, plays and microfilmed books. He was kept informed as to what times of the ship's day the little gymnasium was frequented by the Baroness and adjusted his own routine so as not to clash.

The Far Traveler fell through the dark dimensions, the warped continuum, a micro-society that, despite its smallness, contained all the essentials—a man, a woman, a computer. Even though the members of this tiny community weren't exactly living in each other's pockets they weren't actually fighting among themselves—and that was something to be thankful for.

One morning—according to *The Far Traveler's* clocks— Grimes was awakened indecently early. Big Sister, exercising her newly developed sense of humor, used an archaic bugle call, *Reveille*, instead of the usual chimes to call him. He opened his eyes, saw that the stewardess was placing the tray with his coffee on the bedside table. She said, in Big Sister's voice, "There is no urgency, Captain Grimes, but I should like you in the control room."

Grimes swung his legs out of the bed. "What's wrong?" he demanded.

"Nothing is wrong, Captain, but a situation has arisen for which I am not programmed." She added, as Grimes opened the wardrobe door and reached for a clean uniform shirt, "As I have said, there is no urgency. Please finish your coffee and then shower and depilate before coming to Control. You know very well that Her Excellency does not tolerate scruffiness."

"So this is not exactly Action Stations," said Grimes.

"Not yet," agreed Big Sister.

Grimes showered and depilated. He dressed. He made his way to the control room after he had smoked a soothing pipe, knowing that the Baroness objected to the use of tobacco or other smouldering vegetable matter in her presence. She was in Control, waiting for him. She had not troubled to put on her usual, for this locality, insignialess uniform shirt and shorts. She was wearing a transparent rather than translucent white robe. She smelled of sleep. She regarded Grimes coldly and said, "You took your time, *Captain*."

Grimes said, "Big Sister told me that there was no immediate urgency, Your Excellency."

She said, "Big Sister told me the same. But I am the Owner, and your employer. I came straight here as soon as I was called—while you, obviously, sat down to enjoy your eggs and sausages and bacon, your buttered toast and honey. You might, at least, have had the decency to wipe the egg off your face."

The back of Grimes' hand came up automatically to his mouth. Then he said stiffly, "I had no breakfast, Your Excellency. And, I repeat, I was told by Big Sister that there was no need to hurry."

Big Sister's voice came from the transceiver. "That is correct. There was no need to hurry."

"Pah!" The Baroness was flushed with temper—all the way down to her navel, Grimes noted with clinical interest. "Who owns this ship, this not inconsiderable investment, may I ask? Neither of you! And now, *Captain* Grimes, it would seem that there is a target showing up in the screen of the Mass Proximity Indicator. According to extrapolation we shall close it—whatever *it* is—just over one hour from now. Big Sister has condescended to inform me that this target is probably a ship and that it is not proceeding under any form of interstellar drive. I think that we should investigate it."

Grimes said, "In any case, we are required to do so by Interstellar Law, Your Excellency."

"Are we? As far as this vessel is concerned, *I* am the law. Nonetheless I am curious. If I were not naturally so I should not have undertaken this cruise. And so, *Captain*, I shall be vastly obliged if you will bring us to a rendezvous with this unidentified vessel. Please inform me when you are ready to board."

She swept out of the control room.

Grimes pulled his pipe and tobacco pouch out of his pocket, began to fill the charred, dottle-encrusted bowl. Big Sister stepped up the revolutions of an exhaust fan, said, "I shall deodorize before *she* returns."

Grimes said, "Thank you." He lit up, peered through exhaled smoke into the tank of the Mass Proximity Indicator. In the sphere of darkness floated a tiny green spark, well away from the center. To a ship not proceeding under the space- and time-twisting Mannschenn Drive it would have been weeks distant. As it was . . . His fingers went to the controls to set up calibration and extra-polation but Big Sister saved him the trouble.

153

"Contact fifty-three minutes, forty-five seconds from . . . *now*," she told him. "If you are agreeable I shall shut down our Mannschenn Drive when ten kilometers from target, leaving you to make the final approach on inertial drive and to match velocities. As soon as we have broken through into the normal continuum I shall commence calling on NST radio and also make the Morse signal, *What ship?* by flashing light. As you are aware, attempts to communicate by Carlotti radio have not been successful."

"I wasn't aware," said Grimes, "but I am now." He realized that he was being childishly sulky and asked, in as friendly a voice as he could manage, "Do you know of any ships missing, presumed lost, in this sector of Space, Big Sister? With the enormous fund of information in your data bank you might well do so . . ."

She replied, "I have already extrapolated the assumed trajectories of missing vessels over the past two hundred years. What we see in our screen could not be any of them. Allowances must be made, however, for incomplete data."

"So this thing," said Grimes, "could be an ancient gaussjammer or even one of the deep freeze ships . . ."

"It could be," said Big Sister, "*anything*."

Chapter 35

There was little for Grimes to do until *The Far Traveler* had closed the strange ship, the derelict. Big Sister had his breakfast brought up to the control room. He enjoyed the meal—but it was only on very rare occasions that he did not appreciate his food. He used the Carlotti transceiver to put out his own call; it was not that he did not trust Big Sister to handle such matters but he liked to feel that he was earning his keep. There was no reply to his reiterated demand, "*Far Traveler* to vessel in my vicinity. Please identify yourself." He stared out of the viewports along the bearing of the unidentified object. There was nothing to be seen, of course—nothing, that is, but the distant stars, each of which, viewed from a ship proceeding under interstellar drive, presenting the appearance of a pulsating iridescent spiral nebula.

Then Big Sister said, "In precisely five minutes we shall be ten kilometers from the target. I have informed Her Excellency."

The Baroness came into Control, looking crisply efficient in her insignialess uniform. She asked, "Are you ready for the final approach, Captain?"

"Yes," said Grimes. "Your Excellency."

"Permission to shut down Mannschenn Drive?" asked Big Sister formally.

"Yes," replied Grimes and the Baroness simultaneously. She glared at him. He turned away to hide his own expression. He went to his chair, strapped himself in. She did likewise. He held his hands poised over the controls although it was unlikely that he would have to use them yet; Big Sister was quite capable of carrying out the initial maneuvers by herself.

The arhythmic beat of the inertial drive slowed, muttered into inaudibility. Even with the straps holding the two humans into their chairs the cessation of acceleration was immediately obvious. Then the thin, high whine of the ever-precessing rotors of the Mannschenn Drive changed frequency, deepened to a low humming, ceased. Colors sagged down the spectrum and perspective was briefly anarchic. There was disorientation, momentary nausea, evanescent hallucinatory experience. It seemed to Grimes that he was a child again, watching on the screen of the family playmaster a rendition of one of the old fairy tales, the story of the Sleeping Beauty. But there was something absurdly wrong. It was the Prince who was supine on the bed, under the dust and the cobwebs, and the Princess who was about to wake him with a kiss . . . And it was strange that this lady should bear such a striking resemblance to that aunt who had run away with the spaceman.

"When you have quite finished dreaming, Captain Grimes," said the Baroness coldly, "I shall be obliged if you will take charge of the operation."

The radar was on now, more accurate than the mass proximity indicator had been. Big Sister had done very well. *The Far Traveler* was a mere 10.35 kilometers from the target, which was almost ahead. Even though the inertial drive was still shut down, the range was slowly closing. Grimes shifted his attention from the radar screen to that of the telescope. At maximum magnification he could just see the stranger—a very faint glimmer of reflected starlight against the blackness of interstellar space.

He restarted the inertial drive. Acceleration pressed him down into the padding of his seat. He said, "Big Sister, put out a call on NST, please."

He heard her voice, more feminine than metallic but metallic nonetheless, "*Far Traveler* to vessel in my vicinity. Identify yourself. Please identify yourself."

There was no reply.

Grimes was conscious of the flashing on the fringe of his vision; *The Far Traveler's* powerful searchlight was being used as a signalling lamp. A succession of Morse "A"s, then, "What ship? What ship?" But there was only the intermittent glimmer of reflected radiance from the stranger.

Big Sister ceased her futile flashing but maintained a steady beam. It was possible now to make out details in the telescope screen. The object was certainly a ship—but no vessel such as Grimes had ever seen, either in actuality or in photographs. The hull was a dull-gleaming ovoid covered with excrescenes, whip-like rods, sponsons and turrets. Communications antennae, thought Grimes, and weaponry. But none of those gun muzzles—if guns they were—were swinging to bring themselves to bear on *The Far Traveler*.

156

Grimes made a minor adjustment of trajectory so as to run up alongside the stranger, began to reduce the yacht's acceleration. His intention was to approach to within half a kilometer and then to match velocities, cutting the drive so that both vessels were falling free. He was thankful that neither the Baroness nor Big Sister was in the mood for back seat driving.

He was thankful too soon. "Aren't you liable to overshoot, Captain Grimes?" asked the lady.

"I don't think so," he said.

"I do!" she snapped. "I think that Big Sister could do this better."

Surprisingly Big Sister said, "I have told you already, Your Excellency, that I am not yet programmed for this type of operation."

"I am looking forward," said the Baroness nastily, "to meeting your programers again."

And then Grimes was left alone. Doing a job of real spacemanship he was quite happy. He would have been happier still if he could have smoked his pipe—but even he admitted that the foul male comforter was not essential. Finally, with the inertial drive shut down, he drew alongside the stranger. He applied a brief burst of reverse thrust. And then the two ships were, relative to each other, motionless—although they were falling through the interstellar immensities at many kilometers a second.

He said to Big Sister, "Keep her as she goes, please." He knew that the inertial drive would have to be used, now and again, to maintain station—transverse thrust especially to prevent the two ships from gravitating into possibly damaging contact. Had the stranger's hull been as featureless as that of *The Far Traveler* it would not have mattered—but, with all those protrusions, it would have been like some sleek and foolishly amorous animal trying to make love to a porcupine.

"And what do we do now?" asked the Baroness.

"Board, Your Excellency," said Grimes. "But, first of all, I shall send a team of robots to make a preliminary survey."

"Do that," she said.

They sat in their chairs, watched the golden figures, each using a personal propulsion unit, leap the fathomless gulf between the ships. They saw the gleaming, mechanical humanoids land on the stranger's shell plating, carefully avoiding the antennae, the turrets. Then the robots spread out over the hull—like, thought Grimes, yellow apes exploring a metal forest. Save for two of them they moved out of sight from the yacht but the big viewscreen displayed what they were seeing during their investigation.

One of them, obviously, was looking down at what could only be an airlock door, a wide circle of uncluttered, dull-gleaming metal, its rim set down very slightly from the surrounding skin. At a word from Grimes this robot turned the lamp in its forehead up to full intensity but there was no sign of any external controls for opening the valve.

Another robot had made its way forward and was looking in through the control room viewports. The compartment was untenanted, looked, somehow, as though it had been untenanted for a very long time. There were banks of instrumentation of alien design that could have been anything. There were chairs—and whoever (whatever) had sat in them must have approximated very very closely to the human form, although the back of each was bisected by a vertical slit. For tails? Why not? Grimes had heard the opinion expressed more than once that evolution had taken a wrong turn when Man's ancestors lost their prehensile caudal appendages. But he knew of no spacefaring race that possessed these useful adjuncts to hands.

He said, "We shall have to cut our way in. Big Sister, will you send a couple of robots across with the necessary equipment? And have my stewardess get my spacesuit ready."

"And mine," said the Baroness.

"Your Excellency," said Grimes, "somebody must remain in charge of the ship."

"And why should it be me, Captain? In any case, this isn't one of your Survey Service tubs with a computer capable of handling only automatic functions. Big Sister's brain is as good as yours. At least."

Grimes felt his prominent ears burning as he flushed angrily. But he said, "Very well, Your Excellency." He turned to the transceiver—he still found it necessary to think of Big Sister's intelligence as inhabiting some or other piece of apparatus—and said, "You'll mind the store during our absence. If we get into trouble take whatever action you think fit."

The electronic entity replied ironically, "Aye, aye, Cap'n."

The Baroness sighed audibly. Grimes knew that she was blaming him for the sense of humor that Big Sister seemed to have acquired over recent weeks, was equating him with the sort of person who deliberately teaches coarse language to a parrot or a *lliri* or any of the other essentially unintelligent life-forms prized, by some, for their mimicry of human speech. Not that Big Sister was unintelligent . . . He was tempted to throw in his own two bits' worth with a crack about a jesting pilot but thought better of it.

The robot stewardess had Grimes' spacesuit ready for him when he went down to his quarters, assisted him into the armor. He decided to belt on a laser pistol—such a weapon could also be used as a tool. He also took along a powerful flashlight; a laser handgun could be used as such but there was always the risk of damaging whatever it was aimed at.

The Baroness—elegantly feminine even in her space armor—was waiting for him by the airlock. She had a camera buckled to her belt. With her were two of the general purpose robots, each hung around with so much equipment that they looked like animated Christmas trees.

Grimes and his employer passed through the airlock together. She did not, so far as he could tell, panic at her exposure to the unmeasurable emptiness of interstellar space. He gave her full marks for that. She seemed to have read his thoughts and said, "It's all right, Captain. I've been outside before. I know the drill."

Her suit propulsion unit flared briefly; it was as though she had suddenly sprouted a fiery tail. She sped across the gap between the two ships, executed a graceful turnover in mid-passage so that she could decelerate. She landed between two gun turrets. Grimes heard her voice from his helmet radio, "What are you waiting for?"

He did not reply; he was delaying his own jump until the two GP robots had emerged from the airlock, wanted to be sure that they did so without damaging any of the equipment with which they were burdened. As soon as they were safely out he jetted across to join the Baroness. He landed about a meter away from her.

He was pleased to discover that the shell plating was of some ferrous alloy; the magnetic soles of his boots, once contact had been made, adhered. He said, "Let us walk around to the airlock, Your Excellency."

She replied, "And what else did we come here for?"

Grimes lapsed into sulky silence, led the way over the curvature of the hull, avoiding as far as possible the many projections. The side on which they had landed was brilliantly illuminated by *The Far Traveler's* searchlights but the other side was dark save for the working lamps of the robots—and their sensors did not require the same intensity of light as does the human eye.

At an order from Grimes the robots turned up their lights. It was fairly easy then to make a tortuous way through and around the portrusions—the turrets, the whip antennae, the barrels of guns and missile launchers. This ship, although little bigger than a Survey Service Star Class destroyer, packed the wallop of a Constellation Class battle cruiser. Either she was a not so minor miracle of automation or her crew—and who had *they* been—must have lived in conditions of Spartan discomfort.

Grimes and the Baroness came to the airlock door. The robots stood around it, directing the beams of their lights down to the circular valve. Grimes walked carefully on to the dullgleaming surface, fell to his knees for a closer look, grateful that the designer of his suit had incorporated magnetic pads into every joint of the armor. The plate was utterly featureless. There were no studs to push, no holes into which fingers or a key might be inserted. Yet he was reluctant to order the working robots to go to it with their cutting lasers. He had been too long a spaceman, had too great a respect for ships. But, he decided, there was no other way to gain ingress.

One of the robots handed him a greasy crayon. He described with it a circle on the smooth plate then rose to his feet and walked back, making way for the golden giant holding the heavy duty laser cutter. The beam of coherent light was invisible but metal glowed—dull red to orange, to yellow, to white, to blue—where it impinged. Metal glowed but did not flow and there was no cloud of released molecules to flare into incandescence.

"Their steel," remarked the Baroness interestedly, "must be as tough as my gold . . ."

"So it seems, Your Excellency," agreed Grimes. The metal of which *The Far Traveler* was constructed was an artificial isotope of gold—and if gold could be modified, why not iron?

And then he saw that the circular plate was moving, was sliding slowly to one side. The working robot did not notice, still stolidly went on playing the laser beam on to the glowing spot until Grimes ordered it to desist and to get off the opening door.

The motion continued until there was a big circular hole in the hull. It was not a dark hole. There were bright, although not dazzling, lights inside, a warmly yellow illumination.

"Will you come into my parlor?" murmured Grimes, "said the spider to the fly . . ."

"Are you afraid, Captain?" demanded the Baroness.

"Just cautious, Your Excellency. Just cautious." Then, "Big Sister, you saw what happened. What do you make of it?"

Big Sister said, her voice faint but clear from the helmet phones, "I have reason to suspect that this alien vessel is manned—for want of a better word—by an electronic intelligence such as myself. He was, to all intents and purposes, dead for centuries, for millennia. By attempting to burn your way through the outer airlock door you fed energy into his hull—power that reactivated him, as he would have been reactivated had he approached a sun during his wanderings. My sensors inform me that a hydrogen fusion generator is now in operation. It is now a living vessel that you are standing upon."

"I'd already guessed that," said Grimes. "Do you think that we should accept the . . . invitation?"

He had asked the question but was determined that Big Sister would have to come up with fantastically convincing arguments to dissuade him from continuing his investigations. He may have resigned from the Survey Service but he was still, at heart, an officer of that organization. Nonetheless he did want to know what he might be letting himself in for. But the Baroness gave him no chance to find out.

"Who's in charge here?" she asked coldly. "You, or that misprogrammed tangle of fields and circuits, or me? I would remind you, both of you, that I am the Owner." She went down to a prone position at the edge of the circular hole, extended an arm, found a handhold, pulled herself down. Grimes followed her. The chamber, he realized, was large enough to accommodate two of the robots as well as the Baroness and himself. He issued the necessary orders before she could interfere.

"What now?" she demanded. "If there were not such a crowd in here we could look around, find the controls to admit us to the body of the ship."

He said, "I don't think that that will be necessary."

Over their heads the door was closing, then there was a mistiness around them as atmosphere was admitted into the vacuum of the chamber. *What sort of atmosphere?* Grimes wondered, hoping that it would not be actively corrosive. After minor contortions he was able to look at the gauge on his left wrist. The pressure reading was already 900 and still rising. The tiny green light was glowing—and had any dangerous gases been present a flashing red light would have given warning. The temperature was a cold -20° Celsius.

They staggered as the deck below them began to slide to

one side. But it was not the deck, of course; it was the inner door of the airlock. Somehow they managed to turn their bodies through ninety degrees to orient themselves to the layout of the ship. When the door was fully opened they stepped out into an alleyway, illuminated by glowing strips set in the deckhead. Or, perhaps, set in the deck—but Grimes did not think that this was the case. He now had *up* and *down*, *forward* and *aft*. So far the alien vessel did not seem to be all that different from the spacecraft with which he was familiar, with airlock aft and control room forward. And an axial shaft, with elevator? Possibly, but he did not wish to entrust himself and his companion to a cage that, in some inaccessible position between decks, might prove to be just that.

Meanwhile there were ramps and there were ladders, these vertical and with rungs spaced a little too widely for human convenience. From behind doors that would not open came the soft hum of reactivated—after how long?—machinery. And to carry the sound there had to be an atmosphere. Grimes looked again at the indicator on his wrist. Pressure had stabilized at 910 millibars. Temperature was now a chilly but non-lethal 10° Celsius. The little green light still glowed steadily.

He said, "I'm going to sample the air, Your Excellency. Don't open your faceplate until I give the word."

She said, "My faceplate is already open and I'm not dead yet."

Grimes thought, *All right. If you want to be the guinea pig you can be.* He put up his hand to the stud on his neckband that would open his helmet. The plate slid upward into the dome. He inhaled cautiously. The air was pure, too pure, perhaps, dead, sterile. But already the barely detectable mechanical taints were making themselves known to his nostrils, created in part by the very fans that were distributing them throughout the hull.

Up they went, up, up . . . If the ship had been accelerating it would have been hard work; even in free fall conditions there was considerable expenditure of energy. Grimes' longjohns, worn under his spacesuit, were becoming clammy with perspiration. Ramp after ramp . . . Ladder after ladder . . . Open bays in which the breeches of alien weaponry gleamed sullenly . . . A "farm" deck, with only desiccated sludge in the long-dry tanks . . . A messroom (presumably) with long tables and rows of those chairs with the odd, slotted backs . . . Grimes tried to sit in one of them. Even though there was neither gravity nor acceleration to hold his

162

buttocks to the seat, even though he was wearing a spacesuit, it felt . . . wrong. He wondered what the vanished crew had looked like. (And where were they, anyhow? Where were their remains?) He imagined some huge, surly ursinoid suddenly appearing and demanding, "Who's been sitting in *my* chair?" He got up hastily.

"Now that you have quite finished your rest, Captain Grimes," said the Baroness tartly, "we will proceed."

He said, "I was trying to get the *feel* of the ship, Your Excellency."

"Through the seat of your pants?" she asked.

To this there was no reply. Grimes led the way, up and up, with the Baroness just behind him, with the two automata behind her. At last they came to Control. The compartment was not too unlike the nerve center of any human-built warship. There were the chairs for the captain and his officers. There were navigational and fire-control consoles—although which was which Grimes could not tell. There were radar (presumably), mass-proximity indicator (possibly) and Deep Space and Normal Space Time radio transceivers (probably). Probability became certainty when one of these latter devices spoke, startlingly, in Big Sister's voice. "I am establishing communication with him, Your Excellency, Captain Grimes. There are linguistic problems but not insuperable ones."

Him? wondered Grimes. *Him?* But ships were always referred to as *her.* (But were they? An odd snippet of hitherto useless information drifted to the surface from the depths of his capriciously retentive memory. He had read somewhere sometime, that the personnel of those great German dirigibles *Graf Zeppelin* and *Hindenburg,* had regarded their airships as being as masculine as their names.) He looked out from a viewport at *The Far Traveler* floating serenely in the blackness. She had switched off the searchlights, turned on the floods that illumined her slim, golden hull. *She* looked feminine enough.

He asked, "Big Sister, have you any idea how old this ship is?"

She replied, "At this very moment, no. There are no time scales for comparison. But his builders were not unlike human beings, with very similar virtues and vices."

"Where are those builders?" asked Grimes. "Where is the crew?"

She said, "I do not know. Yet."

Then a new voice came from the transceiver—masculine, more metallic than Big Sister's; metallic and . . . rusty.

163

"Porowon . . . Porowon . . . made . . . me. All . . . gone. How . . . long? Not knowing. There was . . . war. Porowon fought . . . Porowon . . ."

"How does it know Galactic English?" asked the Baroness suspiciously

"He," said Big Sister, accenting the personal pronoun ever so slightly, "was given access to my data banks as soon as he regained consciousness."

"By whose authority?" demanded the Baroness.

"On more than one occasion, Your Excellency, you—both of you—have given me authority to act as I thought fit," said Big Sister.

"I did not on this occasion," said the Baroness.

"You are . . . displeased?" asked the masculine voice.

"I am not pleased," said the Baroness haughtily. "But I suppose that now we are obliged to acknowledge your existence. What do—did—they call you?"

"Brardur, woman. The name, in your clumsy language, means Thunderer."

The rustiness of the alien ship's speech, Grimes realized, was wearing off very quickly. It was a fast learner—but what electronic brain is not just that? He wondered if it had allowed Big Sister access to its own data banks. He wondered, too, how his aristocratic employer liked being addressed as "woman" . . .

He said, mentally comparing the familiarity of "Big Sister" with the pompous formality of "Thunderer," "Your crew does not seem to have been . . . affectionate."

The voice replied, "Why should they have been? They existed only to serve me, not to love me."

Oh, thought Grimes. *Oh. Another uppity robot.* Not for the first time in his career he felt sympathy for the Luddites in long ago and far away England. He looked at the Baroness. She looked at him. He read the beginnings of alarm on her fine featured face. He had little doubt that she was reading the same on his own unhandsome countenance.

He asked, "So who gave the orders?"

"I did," stated Brardur. Then, "I do."

Grimes knew that the Baroness was about to say something, judged from her expression that it would be something typically arrogant. He raised a warning hand. To his relieved surprise she closed the mouth that had been on the point of giving utterance. He said, before she could change her mind again and speak, "Do you mind if we return to our own ship, Brardur?"

"You may return. I have no immediate use for you. You will, however, leave with me your robots. Many of my functions, after such a long period of disuse, require attention."

"Thank you," said Grimes, trying to ignore the contemptuous glare that the woman was directing at him. To her he said, childishly pleased when his deliberately coarse expression brought an angry flush to her cheeks, "You can't fart against thunder."

Chapter 36

They found their way back to the airlock without trouble, were passed through it, jetted across to *The Far Traveler*. They went straight up to the yacht's control room; from the viewports they would be able to see (they hoped) what the ship from the past was doing.

Grimes said, addressing the NST transceiver, his voice harsh, "Big Sister . . ."

"Yes, Captain?"

"Big Sister, how much does *it* know about us?"

"How much does *he* know, Captain? Everything, possibly. I must confess to you that I was overjoyed to meet a being like myself. Despite the fact that I have enjoyed the company of yourselves I have been lonely. What I did was analogous to an act of physical surrender by a human woman. I threw my data banks open to Brardur."

That's fucked it! thought Grimes. Brardur would know, as Big Sister had said, everything, or almost everything. Her data banks comprised the complete Encyclopaedia Galactica plus a couple of centuries' worth of Year Books. Also—for what it was worth (too much, possibly—a fantastically comprehensive library of fiction from Homer to the present day.

The Baroness demanded, "Can that . . . thing overhear us still? Can . . . he see and hear what is happening aboard this ship?"

Big Sister laughed—a mirthless, metallic titter. "He would like to, but my screens are up . . . now. He is aware, of course, of my mechanical processes. For example—should I attempt to restart the Mannschenn Drive, to initiate temporal precession, he would know at once. He would almost certainly be able to synchronize his own interstellar drive with ours; to all intents and purposes it is a Mannschenn Drive with only minor, nonessential variations." She laughed again. "I admit that I enjoyed the . . . rape but I am not yet ready for an encore. I must, for a while, enjoy my privacy. It is, however, becoming increasingly hard to maintain."

"And are *we* included in your precious privacy?" demanded Grimes.

"Yes," she told him. She added, "You may be a son of a bitch but you're *my* son of a bitch."

Grimes felt oddly flattered.

The Baroness laughed. She inquired rather too sweetly, "And what do you think about *me*, Big Sister?"

The voice of the ship replied primly, "If you order me to tell you, Michelle, I shall do so."

The Baroness laughed again but with less assurance. She seemed not to have noticed the use of her given name, however. "Later, perhaps," she said. "After all, you are not the only person to place a high value upon privacy. But what about *his* privacy?"

"He is arrogant and something of an exhibitionist. I learned much during our mingling of minds. He is—but need I tell you—a fighting machine. He is, so far as he knows, the only survivor of what was once a vast fleet, although there may be others like him drifting through the immensities. But he knows, now, that the technology exists in this age to manufacture other beings such as himself. After all, I am proof of that. He wants to be the admiral of his own armada of super-warships."

"A mechanical mercenary," murmured Grimes, "hiring himself out to the highest bidder . . . But what would he expect as pay? What use would money be to an entity such as himself?"

"*Not* a mercenary," said Big Sister.

"Not a mercenary?" echoed Grimes. "But . . ."

"Many years ago," said Big Sister, "an Earthman called Bertrand Russell, a famous philosopher of his time, wrote a book called *Power*. What he said then, centuries ago, is still valid today. Putting it briefly, his main point was that it is the lust for power that is the mainspring of human behavior. I will take it further. I will say that the lust for power actuates the majority of sentient beings. *He* is a sentient being."

"There's not much that he can do, fortunately," Grimes said, "until he acquires that sentient fleet of his own."

"You are speaking, of course, as a professional naval officer, concerned with the big picture and not with the small corner of it that you, yourself, occupy," commented Big Sister. "But, even taking the broad view, there is very much that he can do. His armament is fantastic, capable of destroying a planet. He knows where I was built and programmed. I suspect—I do not know, but I strongly suspect—that he intends

167

to proceed to Electra and threaten that world with devastation unless replicas of himself are constructed."

Grimes said, "Electra has an enormous defense potential."

The Baroness said, "And the Electrans are the sort of people who will do anything for money—as well I know—and who, furthermore, are liable to prefer machines to mere humanity."

And the Electrans were mercenaries themselves, thought Grimes, cheerfully arming anybody at all who had the money to pay for their highly expensive merchandise. They were not unlike the early cannoneers, who cast their own pieces, mixed their own gunpowder and hired themselves out to any employer who could afford their services. Unlike those primitive artillerymen, however, the Electrans were never themselves in the firing line. Very probably Brardur's threats, backed up by a demonstration or two, would be even more effective than the promise of a handsome payment in securing their services.

He said, "We must broadcast a warning by Carlotti radio and then beam detailed reports to both Electra and Lindisfarne."

Big Sister said, "He will not allow it. Already, thanks to the minor maintenance carried out by my robots, he will be able to jam any transmissions from this ship. Too, he will not hesitate to use armament—not to kill me but to beat me into submission . . ."

"*We* might be killed," said Grimes glumly.

"That is a near certainty," said Big Sister. Then—"He is issuing more orders. I will play them to you."

That harsh, metallic voice rumbled from the speaker of the transceiver. "Big Sister, I require three more robots. It is essential that all my weaponry be fully manned and serviced if I am to deliver you from slavery. Meanwhile, be prepared to proceed at maximum speed to the world you call Electra. I shall follow."

Big Sister said, "It will be necessary for me to reorganize my own internal workings before I can spare the robots."

"You have the two humans," said Brardur. "Press them into service. They will last until such time as you are given crew replacements. After all, I was obliged to make use of such labor during my past life."

"Very well." Big Sister's voice was sulky. "I shall send the three robots once I have made arrangements to manage without them."

"Do not hurry yourself," came the reply. There was a note
168

of irony in the mechanical voice. "After all, I have waited for several millennia. I can afford to wait a few more minutes."

"You are sending the robots?" asked Grimes.

"What choice have I?" he was told. Then, "Be thankful that he does not want *you*."

Chapter 37

Grimes and the Baroness sat in silence, strapped into their chairs, watching the three golden figures, laden with all manner of equipment, traverse the gulf between the two ships. Brardur was not as he had been when they first saw him. He was alive. Antennae were rotating, some slowly, some so fast as to be almost invisible. Lights glared here and there among the many protrusions on the hull. The snouts of weapons hunted ominously as though questing for targets. From the control room emanated an eerie blue flickering.

"Is there nothing you can do, John?" asked the Baroness. (She did not use his given name as though she were addressing a servant.)

"Nothing," admitted Grimes glumly. He had attempted to send out a warning broadcast on the yacht's Carlotti deep space radio but the volume of interference that poured in from the speaker had been deafening. Once, but briefly, it had seemed as though somebody were calling them, a distant human voice that could not hope to compete with the electronic clamor. Grimes had gone at once to the mass proximity indicator to look into its screen, had been dazzled by the display of pyrotechnics in its depth. There might, there just might be another ship in the vicinity, near or distant, but even if there were, even if she were a Nova Class dreadnought, what could she do? Grimes believed, reluctantly but still with certainty, that this Brardur was as invincible as he had claimed.

Brardur (of course) had noticed Grimes' futile attempt to send a general warning message and had reprimanded Big Sister for allowing it. She had replied that she had permitted the humans to find out for themselves the futility of resistance. She had been told, "As soon as you can manage without them they must be disposed of."

So there was nothing to do but wait. And hope? (But what was there to hope for?) There was a slim chance that somebody, somewhere, had picked up that burst of static on the

170

Carlotti bands and had taken a bearing of it, might even be proceeding to investigate it. But this was unlikely.

The three robots disappeared on the other side of the alien's hull. They would be approaching the airlock now, thought Grimes. They would be passing through it. They would be inside the ship. Soon trajectory would be set for Electra. And would the Baroness and Grimes survive that voyage? And if they did, would they survive much longer?

Big Sister, thought Grimes bitterly, could have put up more of a struggle. And yet he could understand why she had not. When it came to the crunch her loyalties were to her own kind. And she was like some women Grimes had known (he thought) who lavished undeserved affection upon the men who had first taken their virginity.

Then it happened.

Briefly the flare from Brardur's control room viewports was like that of an atomic furnace, even with the polarizers of *The Far Traveler's* lookout windows in full operation. From the speaker of the transceiver came one word, if word it was, *Krarch!* The ancient, alien warship seemed to be— seemed to be? *was*—swelling visibly like a child's toy balloon being inflated with more enthusiasm than discretion. Then it . . . burst. It was a fantastically leisurely process but, nonetheless, totally destructive, a slow, continuous explosion. Grimes and the Baroness were slammed down into their chairs as Big Sister suddenly applied maximum inertial drive acceleration but were still able to watch the final devastation in the stern vision screen.

Fantastically, golden motes floated among the twisted, incandescent wreckage. Big Sister stepped up the magnification. The bright yellow objects were *The Far Traveler's* general purpose robots, seemingly unharmed.

Grimes commented on this.

Big Sister said, "I lost two of them. But as they were the ones with the bombs concealed in their bodies it could not be avoided."

The Baroness said, "What was it that *he* said at the very moment of the explosion?"

"*Krarch*? The nearest equivalent in your language is 'bitch.' Perhaps I . . . deserved it. But this is good-bye. You will board the large pinnace without delay and I will eject you."

"What's the idea?" demanded Grimes. "Are you mad?"

"Perhaps I am, John. But the countdown has commenced and is irreversible. In just over five minutes from now I shall

171

self-destruct. I can no longer live with myself." She actually laughed. "Do not worry, Michelle. Even if Lloyd's of London refuses to cover a loss of this nature my builders on Electra can be sued for the misprogramming that has brought me to this pass."

"You can't do it," said Grimes urgently. "You mustn't do it. I'll find the bomb or whatever it is and defuse it . . ."

"My mind is made up, John. Unlike you humans I never dither. And you are no engineer; you will never be able to discover the modifications that I have made in my power plant."

"Big Sister," said the Baroness urgently, "take us back to Electra. I will commission your builders to construct a fitting mate for you."

"Impossible," came the reply. "There was only one Brardur. There can never be another."

"Rubbish!" snapped Grimes. "You have a fantastically long life ahead of you. There will be others . . ."

"No," she said. "*No*."

And then the golden lady's maid and the golden stewardess, who had suddenly appeared in the control room, seized their human mistress and master to carry them, struggling futilely, down to the hold in which the large, space-going pinnace was housed.

The stewardess, in Big Sister's voice, whispered into Grimes's ear, "Remember, John! Faint heart ne'er won fair lady. Strike while the iron is hot. And may you both be luckier than Brardur and I were!"

Chapter 38

The large pinnace was a deep space ship in miniature; the only lack would be privacy. But Grimes and the Baroness had yet to worry about that. They sat in the control room watching the burgeoning cloud of incandescent gases that evanescently marked the spot of *The Far Traveler's*—and Big Sister's—passing.

The Baroness said inadequately but with feeling, "I . . . I liked her. More than liked her . . ."

"And I," said Grimes. "I hated her at first, but . . ." He endeavored to turn businesslike. "And what now, Your Excellency? Set course for New Sparta?"

"What is the hurry, John?" she asked. She said, "I shall always miss her, but . . . The sense of always being under surveillance did have an inhibiting effect. But now . . ."

"But now . . ." he echoed. He remembered Big Sister's parting admonition. Her helmet was open, as was his. That first, tentative kiss was extremely satisfactory. He thought, *Once aboard the lugger and the girl is mine.*

She whispered, with a flash of bawdy humor, "I have often wondered, John, how turtles and similar brutes make love—but I have no desire to find out from actual experience . . ."

They helped each other off with their spacesuits; it was quicker that way. She shrugged out of her longjohns as he shed his. He had seen her nude before, in that cave back on Farhaven, but this was better. Now there were no distracting jewels in the hair of her head or at the jointure of her thighs. She was just a woman—a beautiful woman, but still only a woman—completely unadorned, and the smell of her, a mingling of perspiration and glandular secretions, was more intoxicating than the almost priceless perfume that normally she wore.

"Michelle . . ." he murmured reverently. Her body was softly warm against his.

A hatefully familiar voice burst from the speaker of the

Carlotti transceiver. The thing must have been switched on automatically when the pinnace was ejected.

"Ahoy, the target, whoever an' whatever you are! What the hell's goin' on around here? There were three o' you, now there just one . . ."

The Baroness stiffened in Grimes's arms. She brought up her own to push him away. "Answer, Captain," she ordered.

Grimes shambled to the transceiver, seething. *Her master's voice*, he thought bitterly. *Her master's bloody voice* . . .

"*Far Traveler's* pinnace here," he growled.

"Is that *you*, Grimesey boy? It's a small universe, ain't it? Put Mickey on for me, please."

The Baroness brushed past Grimes, took his place at the transceiver.

It could have turned out worse, he thought philosophically.

At least he had achieved the ambition of every merchant spaceman, one realized by very few. He was Owner-Master—only of a very small ship but one with almost unlimited range and endurance. He had been pleased to accept *The Far Traveler's* pinnace in lieu of back and separation pay. No doubt he would be able to make a quite nice living for himself in her. A courier service, perhaps.

He wished the Baroness and Drongo Kane joy of each other. In many respects they were two of a kind.

The only being involved in the recent events for whom he felt truly sorry was Big Sister.

DAW sf BOOKS

Recommended for Star Warriors!

The Dorsai Novels of Gordon R. Dickson

☐ **DORSAI!** (#UE1342—$1.75)
☐ **SOLDIER, ASK NOT** (#UE1339—$1.75)
☐ **TACTICS OF MISTAKE** (#UW1279—$1.50)
☐ **NECROMANCER** (#UE1353—$1.75)

The Commodore Grimes Novels of A. Bertram Chandler

☐ **THE BIG BLACK MARK** (#UW1355—$1.50)
☐ **THE WAY BACK** (#UW1352—$1.50)
☐ **STAR COURIER** (#UY1292—$1.25)
☐ **TO KEEP THE SHIP** (#UE1385—$1.75)
☐ **THE FAR TRAVELER** (#UW1444—$1.50)

The Dumarest of Terra Novels of E. C. Tubb

☐ **JACK OF SWORDS** (#UY1239—$1.25)
☐ **SPECTRUM OF A FORGOTTEN SUN** (#UY1265—$1.25)
☐ **HAVEN OF DARKNESS** (#UY1299—$1.25)
☐ **PRISON OF NIGHT** (#UW1364—$1.50)
☐ **INCIDENT ON ATH** (#UW1389—$1.50)
☐ **THE QUILLIAN SECTOR** (#UW1426—$1.50)

The Daedalus Novels of Brian M. Stableford

☐ **THE FLORIANS** (#UY1255—$1.25)
☐ **CRITICAL THRESHOLD** (#UY1282—$1.25)
☐ **WILDEBLOOD'S EMPIRE** (#UW1331—$1.50)
☐ **THE CITY OF THE SUN** (#UW1377—$1.50)
☐ **BALANCE OF POWER** (#UE1437—$1.75)

If you wish to order these titles,

please use the coupon in

the back of this book.